Neil Flambé

AND THE

CRUSADER'S CURSE

Neil Flambé

AND THE

CRUSADER'S CURSE

KEVIN SYLVESTER

SIMON & SCHUSTER BOOKS FOR YOUNG READERS
New York   London   Toronto   Sydney   New Delhi

SIMON & SCHUSTER BOOKS FOR YOUNG READERS
An imprint of Simon & Schuster Children's Publishing Division
1230 Avenue of the Americas, New York, New York 10020
This book is a work of fiction. Any references to historical events, real people,
or real locales are used fictitiously. Other names, characters, places, and incidents are
products of the author's imagination, and any resemblance to actual events
or locales or persons, living or dead, is entirely coincidental.
Copyright © 2012 by Kevin Sylvester
All rights reserved, including the right of reproduction in whole or in part in any form.
SIMON & SCHUSTER BOOKS FOR YOUNG READERS is a trademark of Simon & Schuster, Inc.
For information about special discounts for bulk purchases, please contact Simon &
Schuster Special Sales at 1-866-506-1949 or business@simonandschuster.com.
The Simon & Schuster Speakers Bureau can bring authors to your live event.
For more information or to book an event, contact the Simon & Schuster Speakers
Bureau at 1-866-248-3049 or visit our website at www.simonspeakers.com.
Book design by Tom Daly
The text for this book is set in Goudy Old Style.
The illustrations for this book are rendered in pen and ink.
Manufactured in the United States of America
0412 FFG
10 9 8 7 6 5 4 3 2 1
Library of Congress Cataloging-in-Publication Data
Sylvester, Kevin.
Neil Flambé and the Crusader's curse / Kevin Sylvester. —1st ed.
p. cm. — ([Neil Flambé capers ; 3])
Summary: The sudden disappearance of fifteen-year-old Neil Flambé's skills as a
world-class chef leads to the closing of his restaurant, a cook-off to save his reputation,
and the discovery of a dark curse that has plagued Flambé cooks for centuries.
ISBN 978-1-4424-4286-3 (hardback)
ISBN 978-1-4424-4297-9 (eBook)
[1. Cooking.—Fiction. 2. Restaurants.—Fiction. 3. Blessing and cursing.—Fiction.
4. Contests.—Fiction. 5. Mystery and detective stories.] I. Title.
PZ7.S98348Nei 2012
[Fic]—dc23
2011044086

To my partner in crime (writing) Laura and our two amazing daughters. If only you liked seafood. Sigh . . .

AND TO EVERYONE . . . KEEP SUPPORTING THOSE FOOD BANKS!

Neil Flambé
AND THE
CRUSADER'S CURSE

Prologue

The Mediterranean, 1225

Pierre stared intently at the horizon. It couldn't be... but it was. He shaded his eyes. Yes, there, bobbing on the sea, was a ship. And it was heading toward the island. The brilliant white sails glimmered in the sun as it sped closer, carried by the warm Mediterranean wind.

Pierre scratched his scraggly beard. He had long since stopped having hallucinations about ships. This had to be happening. Still, he needed to be cautious. As the ship got closer, he could see the flag with the familiar blue circle and cross flying from the ship's mast. He shuddered. A ship flying the exact same flag had dumped him on this miserable rock... when? He struggled to remember how long ago that was, but couldn't.

Pierre remembered the details, though, as clearly as if it were yesterday. It had been the treacherous Jean Valette who'd gleefully shoved him onto the rocky beach, hands and feet still bound, and just as gleefully had thrown one meager sack of barley after him. It had broken open, spilling grains all over the pebbles and stone.

"Feed yourself on that." Valette had sneered. "Once it's gone I guess you'll have to be more creative." He'd said the word "creative" with a twisted smile.

Pierre had looked at the desolate rocky landscape. No herbs, no sheep, no chickens, lambs, cows, or even horses, a gamey meat Pierre had once fed to the Pope himself. There were just a few scrubby bushes and stunted trees. He'd have to be creative indeed if he were to have any chance of surviving. To think Valette had once been Pierre's guardian, his teacher, his mentor. Now he was his executioner.

Valette had turned back into the foaming surf and climbed into the waiting rowboat. As he had sailed away he'd called back, "You are not just a traitor to me, and to the Order, but to God above. We'll see if God can forgive you. I never will." Then he had spat in Pierre's general direction.

Pierre had struggled to stand.

Valette had taken out his knife and thrown it at Pierre's feet. "You can use this to cut your bonds," he said, "and later you can use it to end your suffering."

A sudden gust of wind had come up. It tipped Valette over and into the surf, where the crew scrambled to haul him, soaking and choking, back on board. Pierre had smiled, despite his dilemma. Then the same gust flew over the scattered barley and brought a welcome scent to Pierre's nose. His smile grew as he realized that there wasn't just barley on the beach. A number of other seeds had been mixed into the bag. It was only a tiny glimmer of hope, but for Pierre, it had helped transform his despair into determination—determination to live and to one day escape and exact his revenge. He watched

as Valette's ship disappeared over the horizon and then set to work.

What followed were long months of backbreaking work. He gathered seaweed, whatever dirt and rotting wood he could grab, and built a garden. He carried stones from the beach and built a kind of hermit's cave. And he hoarded the barley, eating as little as possible.

The next spring his work and sacrifice paid off. Tiny green sprouts of fragrant herbs sprouted in his makeshift garden. He protected them from wind and cold, and brought them to maturity. Now he was able to do what he did best: cook.

Pierre speared fish, when the current carried them close enough to shore. He learned to throw stones accurately enough to bring down gulls. It wasn't the best bird flesh in the world, but on the island, it became a welcome feast.

He hadn't thrived, but he hadn't died.

Now, for the first time, a ship headed toward him. Was it a rescue? Or was Valette returning to ensure he'd actually died—and to finish him off if he hadn't? Pierre had a full belly and, thanks to his hard labor, incredibly strong arms and legs. If there was going to be a fight, he was ready. The crew lowered a rowboat into the sea and approached the beach. Pierre hid behind his stone house and clutched the knife. He peered around the wall.

His heart leaped when he saw the man at the standing at the bow of the rowboat. It wasn't Valette. It was his beloved cousin, Lawrence. Pierre hadn't seen him since they'd fought together in the Holy Land. Pierre grimaced at the memory. That campaign was the reason he was here.

Pierre ran out from his hiding place and into the surf before the boat could land.

Lawrence spied the wild-looking man coming toward him and grabbed the hilt of his sword.

"Cousin, it's me! Pierre!" Pierre yelled, splashing right up to the edge of the boat. Lawrence let his grip loosen and an enormous smile spread across his scruffy face.

"Pierre?! Impossible."

Soon they were hugging and laughing and crying. Later, as they sat together on the ship, eating meals from Lawrence's wonderful store of smoked meats and cheeses, they filled in the holes of the story.

"Why did you come for me?" Pierre said at last.

"Things have changed. The Pope and King both gave me permission to come claim your body for a proper burial. Now I see that won't be necessary."

"No thanks to that scoundrel Valette," Pierre said, fingering his knife. "I wonder if he will exile me again once he finds out that I'm alive?"

"Valette is dead," Lawrence said, avoiding Pierre's gaze.

"Why can't you look at me when you bring me such happy news?" Pierre asked.

"Because of his final words."

"What did he say?"

"The priest asked him if he had anything to repent for. Instead of repenting . . . " Lawrence's voice trailed off.

"Yes?" Pierre stood up and grabbed Lawrence's arm.

"Instead of repenting, he used his last breath to utter a curse."

Pierre shook with anger. "What kind of curse? He has already robbed me of so much."

"He said . . . " Lawrence paused, uncertain of how to break the news. "He said that from now until the end of time, no Flambé would ever cook again. If they even tried, they would pay a horrible price. He vowed death itself. Pierre, you must never cook again."

Pierre fell backward, shocked. "Never cook again?" It was the worst curse he could imagine. He pulled a small notebook from his coat. It was the one possession he'd been able to smuggle onto the island, tucked into his stockings. It contained years of recipes, and even dishes he'd only dreamed of and never made. He pored over the words he'd scratched into the parchment with a pen made of gull feather and often his own blood for ink.

"No," he said defiantly. "Never! The Flambés will become the greatest chefs the world has ever known. Curse or no curse!"

A few seconds later, a bolt of lightning hit the mast, and the ship caught fire.

Chapter One

Four and Twenty Thousand Black Birds

Every night, around dinnertime, all the crows in Vancouver fly east, abandoning downtown for the surrounding suburbs and their hills. It's an amazing sight, a sky filled with cawing black birds, moving over the houses and parks like an enormous living storm cloud. No one knows for sure why they do this. Some believe they sense night is coming on, and bad things happen in the city at night.

Neil Flambé, on his fifteenth birthday, burst out of the back door of his kitchen and into the alleyway behind his restaurant, Chez Flambé. He was hyperventilating. His eyes were wide with panic. A crow gave a loud caw and Neil glanced toward the sky. As he gulped desperately for air he watched the birds pass over his head, momentarily blocking out the setting sun. He felt a chill run down his spine, but it wasn't the cool evening air. The dark murder of crows seemed to match his mood perfectly.

Neil took a deep breath and tried to calm down. He could hear the Soba twins back in the kitchen calling in more dinner orders. Neil shook as his sense of rising panic returned. He prided himself on running the kitchen like a finely tuned clock, but it didn't take long for orders to back up—one more disaster he couldn't deal with right now. The crows continued to stream overhead. His foot tingled. Maybe he could just run away? No. Yes. What was going on? "Calm down!" he yelled at himself.

His birthday had not gone well. He'd gotten into fights with his girlfriend, Isabella; his cousin, Larry; and his mentor, Angel. Of course, that wasn't so different from an ordinary day. But what had *just* happened was so shocking he could scarcely believe it.

The first group of customers had arrived early for their dinners at the grand reopening of the newly (and expensively) renovated Chez Flambé. They'd arrived to new tables, new engraved silverware, new linen, new dishes, and wonderful food.

Neil had cooked and served them a dozen of his latest creations, perfectly balanced and chosen for the occasion: mouthwatering mushroom risottos, succulent zucchini flowers stuffed with ricotta cheese and fried in olive oil, perfect pesto and Manchego cheese pizzas. He'd even allowed himself a smile at the thought of the compliments that would soon come flooding back through his gleaming stainless steel kitchen doors.

Instead, what had come back to the kitchen were at least half of the plates.

The customers had sent their dinners back.

Neil had to say it out loud to himself again now to actually believe it. "They sent their dinners back. They sent *my* dinners *back*."

Amber and Zoe, his twin waitresses, had barely whispered the complaints.

"Too salty."

"Too sweet."

"Something tastes off."

"Tastes like a can."

"Over-seasoned."

What? These dishes were prepared by Neil Flambé, not some hack with a hot plate! Neil had sniffed each dish closely. His incredible sense of smell—his secret weapon in the kitchen—had told him that his dishes were exactly as he had intended them. He even stuck his wooden spoon into the risotto and scooped out a huge mouthful.

It was, as he expected, sublime. "Those idiots must be drunk," Neil said.

"I thought the customer was always right," Neil's cousin, Larry, called back from the sink where he was busy washing some carrots and zucchini.

"I thought the sous-chef was always quiet," Neil shot back.

"Yes, chef." Larry sighed and turned his attention back to the vegetables.

Still, Neil had to admit Larry had a point. Customers paid his bills, and those bills were huge. Neil gritted his teeth. "Tell them I'll send a fresh order out ASAP," he hissed to the twins.

Neil prepared the dishes exactly as he had the time

before, sniffing at each tiny step to be certain that the dish was up to his exacting standard. The twins carried out the dishes with Neil's assurance that they were perfect.

But within minutes the dishes had returned again with the same complaints. Neil shook with rage. He grabbed the plates and threw the dishes through his back window, without bothering to open it, sending shards of glass and gourmet food to the cats waiting outside.

Neil cursed. "Calm down, Neil," Larry said.

"Maybe the vegetables are off?" Zoe suggested.

"Or the spices?" Amber said.

Neil shook his head. "Not in a million years. I'm going to go give these idiots a piece of my mind to chew on," Neil spat. He stormed out of the kitchen, sending the double doors swinging violently behind him. He marched toward the seated customers, and stopped dead in his tracks. Neil's nose started twitching. Something was wrong. He sniffed closely. His super-sensitive nose was picking up was the unmistakable odor of . . . glue? The customers turned to see what was going on, then quickly turned their attention back toward their plates.

The men all had beards. The women wore wigs. Larry came up beside Neil. "You okay, chef-boy? I was waiting for the sound of you alienating our clientele. . . ."

Neil started to back away. "They're all in disguise."

"What are they, spies?" Larry asked.

"Worse," Neil whispered. "Food critics." He turned toward the kitchen and quickened his pace. His chest heaved and his head spun. Of course they were critics! This was the grand reopening of the best restaurant in the city, maybe the world. They were here, in disguise, to test the new menu. Neil's throat started to constrict and his chest tightened even more.

This was serious. He didn't just *want* good reviews, he *needed* them. Neil needed these people to spread the word of his skill as thickly as one of his kalamata olive tapenades on a good crostini. But now they had already sent back not one, but two sets of dishes. This was a disaster. He sprinted past Larry, through the kitchen, and out the back door to the alley, where he sat, wondering how this could have happened.

"Neil, where are you?" came Amber's voice through the broken window. "Is everything okay?"

Neil didn't answer. He didn't know what the answer was. Had his nose failed him? His taste buds? Was he . . . losing it? It wasn't unheard of for chefs to burn out, to lose their edge, but he was at the top of his game and he was just fifteen. Was it, gulp, more puberty?

He felt the slight fuzz on his chin as he watched the cats eagerly lap up the discarded food, expertly avoiding the shards of broken window. The cats purred and chewed and purred some more. Neil stopped rubbing his chin. This was interesting. He got up slowly and walked over to where the cats were greedily eating his dinner. These were no ordinary alley cats. Raised on a steady diet of Neil's not-quite-perfect but still pretty amazing culinary rejects, they were almost as discerning as Neil when it came to food. If they were willing to risk sliced tongues to get at his risotto . . . he must be doing something right.

"Good kitty," he said, and patted the fattest cat on the head. Then he stood up straight and turned back toward the kitchen door. "But that's it. No more food tonight." The cats meowed angrily. The crows cawed overhead. Neil watched as the last of them sped off to the mountains and the last rays of sunlight glanced off the rooftops of his neighborhood.

"Time to cook," he said, his lungs now filled with air and determination.

"Um, Neil, we still running a restaurant here?" It was Larry, who held the screen door open to let Neil in.

Neil didn't answer. He marched back into the kitchen, past Larry and straight toward the stove, his face as still as stone. He had to concentrate, cook. Something weird was going on, for sure, but there was no way Neil was going to let it get the best of him. His moment of panic was just that, a moment. Okay, he'd use a little less salt, a little less seasoning, even though everything inside told him he was wrong, but he'd adjust to the critics' demands.

He'd figure out the problem later.

Larry caught the steeled expression on Neil's face.

"Good cheffy," Larry said with a smile, and he let go of the door. "Now, let's cook!"

The screen door banged shut. The noise attracted the cats, who looked lazily up at the faded green wood. One cat cocked his head. Someone had left a strange mark, like a circle and a cross, burned into the door.

There was a yell from inside the kitchen as Neil

struggled to make a slightly seasoned and barely salted order of Pommes de Terre à la Flambé. The cats, as cats do, quickly forgot the mark and licked their lips with each yell. "No more food," the tall redheaded kid in the chef hat had said, but the cats knew better. They sat gazing at the broken window, and waited.

Chapter Two

Carrion Laughing

Neil slumped down on the sidewalk outside Chez Flambé, his back against the painted tile. He hung his head. He wanted to moan, but wasn't sure he had the energy. His clothes were soaked with sweat. He was absolutely exhausted. Cooking tonight hadn't been a pleasurable challenge, but a grueling battle. Neil had to work against his instincts, his expertise, in a maddening attempt to please the incognito critics.

"I can't believe how little sea salt I ended up putting in my mushroom bisque." He shook his head sadly. At least the critics hadn't sent the third round of dishes back . . . but Neil knew it wasn't his best work. That was unforgivable. He still wasn't sure what had gone wrong.

"It just makes no sense!" he mumbled.

"They should have been asking for seconds, not leaving food on their plates."

Neil had even announced to everyone that dinner was on the house. That was a financial hit he couldn't really afford, but he hoped it might eke out some measure of compassion from the critics before they savaged him in the coming weekend's papers.

"Darn," he said, lowering his head into his palms. "That could not have gone any worse."

"Well, happy birthday," Larry said, sitting beside him. "I did get you this."

"A time machine, I hope."

"Um, no. I'm thinking of the future." Larry handed Neil a tiny box, wrapped in a scrap of that morning's newspaper.

"It's some white truffle oil from Northern Italy," Larry said with a smile.

"Seriously?"

Larry nodded.

"That's actually really . . . nice," Neil said. He carefully opened the package. A small glass vial containing a golden liquid fell into his palm.

"And it's the really good stuff too," Larry said, beaming.

Neil began to smile, but stopped. He looked sideways at Larry. "Wait a minute. This is the good stuff . . . and it isn't cheap. How did you— Wait, never mind. I don't want to know. The less I know, the less chance there is that I can testify in court."

Larry chuckled. "Don't worry, Sirloin

Holmes, nothing weird about this
one. I had a friend who was heading over to Italy for school."

"Let me guess. SHE owed
you a favor?"

"Not a favor, exactly. She
just wanted to say thanks."

"For?"

"Never mind," Larry
said with a faraway look in his
eye and a smile.

Neil watched the liquid
sparkle in the soft light of Chez
Flambé. Expensive, rare, and
exquisite, truffle oil like this
should go in a special dish and
should be used soon, while it was
still fragrant and fresh. But could
he risk it? What if he wasted it on
dishes that got sent back? He found the
energy to moan and let his head slump.

"I thought you said birthdays were lucky," Neil said
quietly. "In fact, I distinctly remember you saying that
on the plane ride back from Mexico City."

"Well, not all luck is good luck," Larry said. "So,
technically, I'm still right."

"Gee, thanks," Neil mumbled between his fingers.

"Besides, isn't Angel always saying you need to find
happiness inside?"

"What does that have to do with anything?"

"Well, *you* know you cooked good food. . . ."

"Great food."

"Whatever." Larry rolled his eyes. "Anyway, Angel always says you need to find happiness from your own self, not from what others say about you. That includes critics."

"The last thing Angel said to me today was 'grow up.'"

"Actually, I think his actual last words were 'shut up.'"

Neil spread his fingers and glared at his cousin. "And?"

"Maybe you shouldn't have been so critical of the frosting he made for your birthday cake."

Neil didn't say anything. Neil could still taste the iodine from the cake. It had tasted bitter, like it had been made with salt instead of sugar. Neil knew, or at least had thought, that Angel would like honest feedback from a great chef. Apparently not.

Larry suddenly laughed and slapped Neil on the back "Hey! How ironic! You sent Angel's cake back. See, it happens to the best chefs . . . like Angel."

Neil ignored the jab.

"It doesn't happen to me," Neil said. He was silent for a moment, thinking. "Those critics must have been up to something,"

"What do you mean?"

"Why would they send them back?"

"Because they tasted like—wait . . . was it cardboard or tin cans?"

"No. Those dishes were perfect. They were perfect. It had to be some ulterior motive. Maybe they were intentionally trying to set me off?"

"Um, okay, why exactly?"

"Because they're jealous? Because they want to tear me down?"

"Um, Neil, maybe you should take a deep breath and settle yourself into a nice calm cup of tea or something."

"Tea?"

"It goes great with humble pie, which is what you're going to be eating if you don't settle down. Critics are critics. They can't like everything you cook."

Neil scoffed. "Of course they can." He stared off into the distance.

"Maybe they've been paid off by some other chef?" Neil said, biting his nail. "They show up to rattle me, send the dishes back, then rip me in the papers." A slight breeze came up and jostled the newspaper Neil had let fall to the ground. Something caught his eye. He cocked his head and looked closely at the page. Tucked next to a story about a piano-playing chipmunk was a tiny advertisement.

> Opening soon. Carrion. Vancouver's
> Newest and Best Restaurant. Look
> for us across from Trader Bob's Only a
> Dime and the Rough dollar store on
> Stella Street.

Trader Bob's on Stella Street? That was right next to . . . Chez Flambé?!

Neil's head snapped up. Across the street stood the derelict remains of the Pets and Pelts kennel and haberdashery. It had been empty and crumbling since way before Neil moved into his place—thank goodness. Neil shoved the truffle oil into his pocket and ran over. There, taped to the inside of the cracked window, was a building permit, reading "Zoned for restaurant." The ad said "opening soon," but Neil couldn't see any sign of work. No wonder he didn't know there was a restaurant coming. Neil pushed his nose against the glass and peered inside. It was almost completely dark. But Neil thought he could see a faint blue light in the gloom, like two eyes staring back at him. Maybe it was a bit of the streetlight reflecting off some metal. A new stove maybe? He blinked and peered inside again, but the light, whatever it was, had disappeared.

Neil stood back and looked at the graffiti-covered walls. A new restaurant? Here? The closest Neil had to competition in this part of town was the falafel and french fry joint that was only open on weekends, four doors down. Neil didn't even consider it competition for his business—more of a danger for his customers. His main concern was that the wind would carry the smell of the putrid fat into his dining room just as he was serving his duck terrine.

Something scurried past his feet, emerging—he was sure—from some crack in the facade of the building. Someone was going to start a restaurant here, to go head-to-head with Neil? Who was the chef? "What idiot would put a restaurant in this part of town?" Neil said angrily.

As if on cue, Larry came up beside him. "Hey, cool, another restaurant!"

Neil gritted his teeth. "Yes, cool . . . another restaurant in a part of town that can barely attract enough customers for ONE! At least I know which chef was paying off those critics. Whoever is starting this place!"

"Well, maybe. But we don't even know who this chef is, or what this place is. It looks haunted. Maybe it's going to be a coffee shop run by animal ghosts!" Larry said with a wide-eyed smile.

"Dream on," Neil said.

"Oh, I will. Coffee served by ghostly rabbits. That would be awesome."

"You are right about one thing. We don't know who's behind any of this, but I intend to find out." Neil grabbed his cell phone and flipped it open. "I'm calling Nakamura."

"Whoa, whoa, cuz, does this really seem like a police emergency?" Larry said, putting his hand on Neil's arm. He did his best imitation of Neil and Sean Nakamura, Neil's frequent partner in solving food-related crimes. "'Nakamura, stop chasing that bank robber.' 'Why, Nose, what's the situation?' 'My food sucked tonight and I think it might be the ghosts of the pets from across the street messing with my marjoram. . . .'"

Neil yanked his arm away. "Get your hands off me!" Neil looked at Larry with an almost crazed expression. Larry was so alarmed he took a step back. Neil caught himself and shook his head. "Sorry, Larry, sorry . . . I'm just a little . . . frazzled."

"Little? You looked a bit more than a little frazzled there, chef-boy."

Neil flipped his phone shut.

"I said I'm sorry. You're right. It's not an emergency," Neil said. "I guess it can wait until tomorrow . . . tomorrow morning."

Larry put his hand back on Neil's shoulder. "Maybe you should get some sleep. I'll finish cleaning up." Neil nodded.

Together, they walked back to Chez Flambé. "Oh, I almost forgot," Larry said. "Your mom and dad dropped by to wish you a happy birthday."

"What? I didn't see them."

"You were busy."

"Doing what?"

"Cooking . . . and yelling. They stuck their heads in the kitchen, but figured you weren't in the mood to be disturbed."

"They couldn't stay?" Neil fought to suppress the slight tremor in his voice.

"Your dad said something about a conference call or a meeting or something. He said they'd see you at home . . . maybe tomorrow." Larry winced as he relayed the message. There was no question Neil's parents loved him, but they weren't exactly the warm-and-fuzzy types.

"Happy birthday to me," Neil said quietly as they walked into the dining room.

"They did leave you this," Larry said, holding a small plain parcel, wrapped in twine. "At least I think they left it."

"What do you mean 'think'? They didn't hand it to you?"

"Well, I only said a quick hello and then had to grab that order of steaks off the grill. It was on the counter after they left and I'm sure it wasn't there before that."

"Great, thanks," Neil said.

"Aren't you going to open it?" Larry asked.

Neil stared at the package. The paper was crinkled and old. The twine looked more like a dirty old shoelace. Typical. "No. I don't think so." Neil walked over to the tiny office at the back of the kitchen and threw the package on top of his desk. It hit some papers and slid off, landing somewhere on the floor with a thud. Neil slammed the office door. "Maybe tomorrow . . . you know, just to prolong such a great birthday."

Larry pumped his fist in the air. "Hey, we'll storm back, big guy. Now get some rest."

Neil grabbed his keys off the wall. He smacked his head. "I forgot. I have English homework due Monday. What else could go wrong?"

As if on cue, it began to rain.

"Let me guess," Larry said, doing his best to suppress a chuckle. "No rain gear?"

Neil didn't say anything. He walked past Larry, out the back door, and climbed onto his increasingly wet bike. Then he pedaled sadly and wetly home.

My dearest Irina,

I can no longer accept my fate, a fate of my own making.

I am leaving you this book. It is the only good thing I have left.

Farewell.

Pierre 1272   1311

Pierre Flambé stared through the rain at his wife and children, sitting around the fire inside of their makeshift home. Pierre didn't have the energy to cry; he let the rainwater wet his cheeks in place of tears. He was a hollow man, defeated . . . cursed.

His family didn't know it, but he was saying good-bye. Pierre had tried to make a life for them. He had failed. He loved his family, and he loved his beautiful Irina. He had loved her ever since that day he had crawled onto the salty shoreline of Malta, his rescue ship smoldering and sinking on the horizon.

She had pulled him away from the waves and had nursed him back to health with meals of honey and cakes and tea made with bitter herbs. Pierre had been able to salvage only one possession from the wreck—his recipe book. He was clutching it when he washed ashore. Irina had to wrench his fingers loose before she could hang it to dry. When he'd

woken from his stupor, he'd panicked, worrying that it had been lost.

The book contained what was left of his life as a wizard with food. The sea had washed away many of the recipes. His blood was not a very waterproof ink. But the marks from the homemade quills could still be read if the page was wetted.

Pierre married Irina, had two wonderful children, and made a living as a cook for a series of lords and ladies and bishops.

Then, one day, for no reason, he lost his ability to cook. He poisoned an influential cardinal. The cardinal had almost died, and wasn't happy. He exiled Pierre from Malta forever. Pierre tried to find cooking jobs elsewhere, but every time he made a new start—began to recover his earlier expertise with food—something horrible would happen. Soon the name Flambé was synonymous with bad food, and hiring Pierre was not a risk anyone was willing to take.

Pierre tried his hand at other jobs, but his heart wasn't in it. A Flambé was meant for greatness. Let the village idiots do the blacksmithing, masonry, and carpentry, he thought bitterly. His body and mind were not meant for these menial things. But he had to feed his family, so he sacrificed his principles and continued with whatever work he could find. Oh, why had be angered Valette? Why had he helped the so-called enemy . . . No, it was too painful to think about the life he might be enjoying now if he'd made different decisions twenty years ago.

Then one day, by some miracle, his cousin Lawrence reappeared. Pierre had assumed Lawrence had drowned in the wreck. Instead, he, too, had washed up on shore after the wreck, but miles away on the coast of Italy. He'd attempted to track Pierre down for years, and was shocked when he saw

the shell of man who was once his younger cousin toiling as a tanner in a leather-maker's shop in LaRochelle.

He tried, without success, to cajole Pierre out of his depression.

Pierre remembered all of this as the rain continued to pelt his scraggly red hair. Lawrence came up beside him.

"Take care of them," Pierre said.

Lawrence was neither shocked nor confused. He knew his cousin was defeated. Lawrence nodded. "I will, I promise."

Pierre pulled out his book and a quill. He scratched a note into the margins of his most precious recipes, then handed the book to Lawrence. Without another word Pierre turned around and disappeared into the nearby woods, and was never seen again.

Chapter Three

Frosty Icing

Angel Jícama sat down at his kitchen table and stared at the birthday cake with a critical eye. It was shaped like a giant chef's hat, with red-hair icing sticking out underneath. He stroked his beard and hummed meditatively. It was a silly cake, he knew, but Neil was so serious all the time and Angel had been hoping to lighten his mood. He hadn't.

Isabella Tortellini and her bodyguard, Jones, sat across from him and stole sideways glances at each other. They had tracked Angel down at his apartment after their disastrous attempt at a birthday party at Chez Flambé. He had invited them in for dinner and tea. Dinner had been great—quail eggs on brown butter toasts—but Angel had been either watching the cake or stabbing it with a knife for a full fifteen minutes now.

"I think it's safely dead," said Jones, keeping a close

eye on the knife. "That tea must be as thick as mud by now," he whispered to Isabella.

Isabella had been keeping a closer eye on Angel's expression. "Angel," she said, reaching across the table and gently touching Angel's hand. "It's getting late. I need to go soon. Is everything okay?"

Angel had been so lost in his own thoughts that he'd almost forgotten that he had guests. "Sorry about that, Isabella," he said. "I'm just a little rattled."

"You can't possibly tell me you're surprised that Flambé kid is a rude little—" Jones started. Isabella gave a little cough and he stopped. "Well, you can't be surprised that he's cocky."

"No. I'm worried because he was wrong about the cake." Angel cut a small slice and placed it on a plate. He stared at it, not offering any to his guests or trying it himself.

Isabella knew why he was being so cautious. This cake had been the cause of a huge blowup between Neil and everyone else earlier at Chez Flambé.

Angel had made a mocha-chocolate-cream bombe for Neil—who had blurted out a short "thanks" but was, predictably, too preoccupied with dinner prep for much else. "Look, skip the candles and song; I've got to work," he'd said. Then he'd sunk a fork into the cake and grabbed a bite.

He immediately spat it out all over the dining room floor. "Angel, that's horrible! What did you do, replace the corn oil with motor oil?" Angel just sat there open-mouthed as Neil turned to Larry. "Clean up this mess. The customers will be here soon."

Neil stormed back into the kitchen and Angel stormed out with the remainder of the cake, after throwing a few choice words in Neil's direction. Isabella stormed into the kitchen herself and chastised Neil for being so rude. He turned on her with an anger she had never seen before. "Are you questioning my skills as a chef? Seriously? Me? I just won a major competition in Mex—"

He stopped when he saw the cold look in her eyes.

"I know there is much pressure on you today, Neil," Isabella had said, poking a finger in Neil's face. "But don't you ever speak to me like this again, or I will never speak to you again." Isabella had a long history of keeping her promises. She had once gone a decade without speaking to a single chef. Only an amazing meal from Neil Flambé had broken that silence. But she was perfectly willing to put a cork back in that perfume bottle.

Neil apologized.

Still, an icy chill had spread over the whole affair. Neil finally said, "I really do need to prep for dinner. I'll call or . . . maybe see you later?"

Isabella hadn't answered. She walked out and then she and Jones had gone in search of Angel.

Now the cake sat between them, saying nothing. She wished it could. Was Angel reacting this way because Neil had been right about the cake? Or maybe it was something else. Angel had worked alongside Neil in the *Azteca Cocina* in Mexico City and had worried that competing would bring back his old demons— his drive for perfection at all costs. Was that why Angel was so angry?

Angel didn't look angry now, though, just worried. He finally took a fork and broke a corner off the slice, making sure to have both icing and cake in the same mouthful. He carefully chewed the piece and swallowed.

"Worse than I thought," he said, laying the fork down on the table and sitting back in his chair. He looked like he wanted to blow the cake up with his stare.

"It tastes that bad?" Isabella said, trying to decipher the look on his face.

"Try for yourself." Isabella reached for a fork. Jones flinched and reached for her arm. Neil Flambé might be a bit of a jerk, but he also had an amazing nose for food that had gone off. Jones had a bodyguard's suspicious nature and Angel had a shady past.

"Um, maybe in a bit."

Isabella pushed his hand away. "Oh, don't worry so much, you suspicious man."

"Suspicion didn't kill any cats, curiosity did," Jones said, but he pulled his hand back.

Isabella took a mouthful. "Oh, my," she said. "Angel, it tastes wonderful."

Angel nodded. "I know." He stood up abruptly and walked to the door. He opened it and stepped aside. "I apologize, but if you two will excuse me, I have to make a very important phone call and I'm afraid I need to be discreet."

"Oh, yes, of course," Isabella said, standing up and wrapping herself in her shawl. "We will call you later, or perhaps see you tomorrow?"

"Perhaps," Angel said.

As soon as the door clicked behind them, Isabella put her ear to the door.

"What are you doing?" Jones whispered.

"Shhh," she said. She waved for Jones to walk down the stairs. He shook his head at her but she just waved more vigorously. He sighed and walked down the stairs. Isabella held her breath and listened closely at the door.

She heard Angel

pushing buttons on his phone, then his voice, way too loud for any kind of private call. "Hello, Pizza Pizzaz? I'd like a giant pizza, with a giant serving of pepperoni and a bushel of lavender."

Pizza with lavender? Isabella pursed her lips and stood up. She'd been caught. She knew Angel's sense of smell was second only to Neil's, but she hadn't known he could smell through closed doors.

"Nice try, Isabella," Angel called out. "Now please go. This call is important."

"Humph," Isabella said. "Fine," she called back. Then she turned and marched noisily down the stairs and out the door. Jones was leaning against the car, smiling, or, as Larry once described it "scowling with an upward curve at the edges. He makes the Mona Lisa look like she's losing it."

Jones opened the car door and let her in. She frowned. "Next time we visit Angel's, remind me NOT to wear perfume."

Chapter Four

Back in the Griddle

Neil Flambé parked his bike behind his restaurant. About a dozen chubby cats were dozing happily next to the dumpster. Neil shook his head at the size of them. The fatter they were, the more trouble he was having with his cooking. He let out a deep sigh.

Finally he was on his home turf, his restaurant where he was able to do what he wanted, and how he wanted to do it (which was perfectly). School had always been hard, and was getting harder. He just wasn't able to concentrate on the area of a parallelogram and what it has to say about the use of metaphor in *The Scarlet Letter*. Maybe that was two different classes melding together, he wasn't sure. He'd been preoccupied with how to turn his cooking around.

Not that he had any idea what was wrong.

As he'd expected, the critics had blasted him in the papers. The free meal and his reputation must have counted for something because he did get three out of four stars from one of the reviewers, but even that was devastating news. The full effect hadn't been felt . . . yet.

Chez Flambé was still full on the weekend. No one returned their dishes, but there was no applause, no slaps on the back or calls for the chef to come say hello. The Soba twins said they could tell something was still off because the tips were smaller. If this kept up they might ask for a raise. Neil shuddered.

And, as if cooking woes and geometry weren't enough, there was also the return of Billy Berger. The class bully had spent the summer in a juvenile detention center for his small part in the case of the Marco Polo murders. In an alternate universe Billy went to the center vowing to turn things around, volunteered at the cafeteria, discovered a love for food and came back to school energized and ready to help the school cook make healthy meals for his smiling fellow students.

In *this* reality Billy joined the detention center's boxing team and ate twice as many Cheez Doodles. He slowly pounded his fist in his palm every time Neil passed him in the hallway. "Like his jail time was my fault!" Neil had yelled to his mother after his first day back.

"Yes, dear," his mother had said. "Play nice with the other children. Bullies are just after attention."

Honestly, sometimes talking to his parents was like talking to a wall. His mom was a busy lawyer, his dad an ad executive. They had zero interest in food, and, he sometimes felt, almost as little interest in their only son. Maybe he should hire them so he could talk to them on their time—billable hours, they called it. Of course, money was yet another worry on his mind. Then there was his lack of sleep. It was probably the stress, but Neil was having a horrible time. He would wake up at all hours of the night, and take even longer to fall back to sleep, if he fell back at all. Sleep was a precious commodity in his life at the best of times, and this was definitely NOT the best of times.

But all those concerns washed away when he entered his kitchen and began prepping for the week's meals. Today was a Monday. Chez Flambé was closed. This was a day for experimenting with new ideas and losing himself in his passion.

He reached for the handle of the screen door and stopped. He could see the circle and cross that someone had burned onto the wood. The shape was tweaking something in his memory, but he couldn't place it. Maybe it was a tag like the sorts he'd seen spray-painted all over the walls in this part of town.

"Stupid kids," Neil said.

"Talking to yourself again?" Larry said, walking up behind Neil and making him jump. "I know you've been stressed a lot lately, but no one wants to have a nutty chef cooking for them. They have nutty allergies . . . get it?"

Neil hadn't heard Larry coming, which was highly unusual. "Where's your obnoxious motorcycle?" Neil said.

"Sold it."

"You're kidding."

"Nope, I needed some cash for my big idea." Larry stood there beaming.

Neil waited for a few seconds to pass before saying, "Which is?"

"My shirt."

Neil looked at Larry's shirt. It was red, smelled like cotton (and coffee), and was otherwise normal, and plain.

"It's a shirt. Nice work, genius."

"The big idea is what it says," Larry said, pointing at the shirt.

Neil looked again. "It doesn't say anything."

"Exactly! That's what I want you to think."

"So your big idea is a plain red shirt and annoying conversation?"

"No. It says something but it's written on the inside."

"The inside?"

"I call it a *me-shirt*. The slogan is on the inside. Only the person wearing it knows what it says. Brilliant, eh?"

Neil rubbed his temples. "I hesitate to ask this. What does your me-shirt say?"

"'I'm with grumpy.'"

Neil frowned. "Don't quit your day job. Wait. On second thought, PLEASE quit your day job."

"Ha, ha. Of course, this is also a fallback plan if the restaurant goes belly-up."

Neil grabbed the screen door violently. "We're not going belly-up! We're just going up!"

"Hey, that's pretty good. Can I put that on a me-shirt?"

"NO! Now let's get to work or *you'll* be going belly-up." Neil yanked the door so hard it almost came off its hinges. The inside door was unlocked and swung open.

"What the heck?" Neil said. Pots and pans and food were strewn all over the counter and floor. He stepped inside. The freezer door was open. The door to the office had been smashed as well. Neil walked over. All the papers had been thrown onto the floor and the drawers jimmied open and emptied.

Larry came up behind him and let out a low whistle. "Wow, someone was looking for something."

Neil looked up on top of the filing cabinet. "Oh NO!" he shrieked. "The safe! It's gone!"

Neil's safe held a number of business papers—but much more importantly, it also contained his favorite recipes and the locations of some of his most carefully guarded suppliers. Its loss would be a disaster.

Neil flipped open his phone and dialed Nakamura.

Nakamura answered on the first ring, and was clearly annoyed. "I told you, Nose, I have no leads yet on who owns that place across the street. Now stop bugging me. I have real crimes to solve."

"I have a real crime. Someone ransacked my kitchen."

"Or Larry didn't clean up again."

"THEY STOLE MY SAFE!" Neil yelled. "IS THAT

A SERIOUS ENOUGH CRIME FOR YOU?"

"Ouch. Thanks for unclogging my ear wax. Fine. I'll be right over."

No sooner did he hang up than there was a knock at the front door.

Neil ran to let the Inspector in. It wasn't Nakamura. Instead, an impeccably dressed man with a mustache stood at the door. He turned to face Neil with a polite nod.

"Neil Flambé. We meet again," said Jean-Claude Chili.

MY SON,

WHEN KING JOHN DIED I HAD
TO RUN.

I HAD NO CHOICE.

PROTECT THIS BOOK AT ALL
COSTS.

IT CONTAINS GOLDEN TREASURE
SPUN FROM MEAGER LEAD.

NICHOLAS 1345   1365

Nicholas Flambé stood in the mud and watched as the King and his soldiers rode through the stone gates of the hunting lodge. Nicholas smiled. The King alone had two stags and three large geese straddled across his horse's back.

"Chef Flambé, time for a feast!" the King said, dismounting next to him.

Nicholas bowed low. "I will bring honor to your name."

"Let us hope I was not wrong to take a chance on such a young chef." The King slapped him hard on the back and strode off toward the house.

Nicholas watched him go. He remembered the first time he had cooked for the King. It had been his own fifteenth birthday, just a few years ago. The King's private chef had taken ill. Nicholas had been a mere helper in the kitchen, but stepped forward and made a meal that left the King speechless. The old chef soon recovered but Nicholas had won himself a job as the chef at the hunting lodge. He wanted more, and now he had his chance.

Nicholas would create a feast that would leave the King no choice but to take him back to the royal court as head chef.

He began yelling at the servants. "Take everything to the kitchen. Skin the stags and take the plumage from these birds. Hurry!"

Nicholas was so busy he didn't notice the strange knight who rode through the gates, a circle and cross painted on his shield. That also meant he didn't notice the same knight's absence from the banquet.

And what a banquet it was. Nicholas prepared a succulent assortment of venison stews, breads, cheeses, and roasts. The King and his knights set upon the food with the wild fury of an army that hadn't eaten in months. The dining hall echoed with satisfied belches and sighs.

Nicholas went to bed with a huge smile, his wife asleep at his side. All that talk of a curse was surely just family legend, he thought as he slipped into a wonderful sleep.

Nicholas woke with a start a few hours later. Someone was knocking at his chamber door.

He got out of bed and ran over to lift the latch. His cousin Loretta, the Queen's private nurse, ran inside and closed the door quickly behind her.

"Nicholas, you must take everything and leave. The King is gravely ill. Three knights have died in the night."

"Died?"

"Murdered?"

"By whose sword?"

"They were . . . poisoned," Loretta said slowly, staring

intently at Nicholas, her usual sense of humor entirely gone. "The King is sick in bed as well, and gravely ill."

Nicholas felt a chill run down his spine.

"My wife is with child," he said. Loretta knew exactly what Nicholas meant. His wife couldn't follow where Nicholas needed to go.

Loretta nodded. "I will protect her."

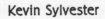

There were footsteps on the stairs. Nicholas grabbed his satchel of knives and his family notebook and jumped from the window and ran and ran and ran.

Nicholas knew that every soldier and sheriff would be ordered to kill him on sight so he kept to the woods.

He hunted and cooked whatever he could find. He became adept at making wonderful meals from horrible ingredients—he wrote many of the recipes down in the notebook—but his new life was taking its toll. A deep cough rattled in his chest. The wounds on his hands and knees no longer healed.

One day he found himself alone on the branch of an ancient oak tree. He clutched a sharpened branch in his right hand, praying for a rabbit to wander underneath, or a squirrel, or even a rat . . . anything edible would do.

A twig cracked.

Something large was moving in the bushes. Nicholas drew his arm back, prepared to strike.

A cloaked figure emerged into the clearing.

Nicholas gasped.

It was Loretta.

"Nicholas. I have news. Are you here?" she called.

Nicholas remained absolutely still. Perhaps it was a trap. Perhaps Loretta had been forced to lure him out into the open.

"Nicholas, you have a son."

Nicholas could feel tears welling in his eyes. He sat up and immediately began to cough.

"Nicholas!" Loretta called, looking up at the tree.

Nicholas tried to speak but could only cough. Blood rose to his lips. Then a searing pain tore through his body. His fingers went slack and the spear fell to the ground. Unable to hold the branch, he fell after it.

Loretta ran to him.

"Nicholas, oh, Nicholas," was all she could say.

Nicholas looked up at her and gave a weak smile. "A son." He coughed again, his body convulsing violently. With his last bit of strength Nicholas reached into his jacket and pulled out the notebook. "You must give him this. And write a note inside . . ." His voice trailed off to barely a whisper.

Loretta leaned close and Nicholas dictated his note. When she raised her head again, he was gone.

Chapter Five

A Chili Reception

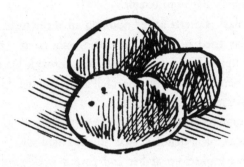

"Who's the nerd?" Larry said, as Neil led Jean-Claude Chili into the messy kitchen of Chez Flambé.

In a wink Chili grabbed a knife from the counter and leaped right up to Larry. He grabbed his ponytail and prepared to slice it off with the knife.

"How would you like zees naird to give you an 'aircut with zees knife, *mon vieux*?"

Larry's eyes grew wide. Then the corners of his mouth began to twitch. Neil took a step forward to defend his cousin, but stopped when Larry gave out an enormous laugh.

"That . . . was . . . the COOLEST thing I have ever seen! You have got to be Jean-Claude Chili. Am I right?"

Chili let go of Larry's ponytail, took a step back and gave a polite bow. "*Oui.*"

"Wow. Neil told me all about you. You were an Olympic fencer, then you were a food critic—"

"He still is a food critic," Neil said, with a sense of foreboding. Why had Chili suddenly appeared at his doorstep?

"—and you saved Neil that time by fending off Carlotta Calamari with a butter knife!"

"Eet was not so difficult to do . . . zees thing you describe," Chili said with a modest wave of his hand. "Eet eez not as difficult as finding zee best chef in zee world, for example."

Neil felt his heart fall. So that's why Chili was here—to test him. Why did Chili have to come visit him now? Why not two months ago when he was wowing everyone with his latest *chilli con cueso*, or in a couple of weeks when he certainly would have figured out what was going wrong with his cooking?

Chili turned to face Neil. "Neil Flambé. I need you to cook for me. Three dishes should suffice. Your best three, eef you please." Then, without a word of explanation, Chili bowed again and took a seat in the dining room. Neil watched through the round window as Chili pulled out his red notebook—the emblem of the Michelin guide critic, the most famous food guide in the world. He opened the book and carefully placed it on the table in front of him. Chili cocked his wrist to check the time, jotted it down in his book, and then lifted his head and smiled a brief smile at Neil. Then he folded his hands on the table and waited.

Neil turned around quickly, his heart racing. "Larry, get on the phone to Gunter Lund and tell him we need a salmon, a really fresh wild salmon, right away."

"Aye aye, captain," Larry said, saluting.

Neil knew one of the many things Chili would judge him on was the speed and efficiency of the service. The food should taste good and it should arrive when the customer was hungry and happy, not famished and frustrated.

"That salmon won't get here for at least ten minutes," Neil said, thinking out loud. "What are we going to serve him until then?"

"Your potatoes?" Larry called back.

"Yes, but something else. Something wonderful."

Suddenly, Neil remembered the truffle oil Larry had given him for his birthday. It was in his backpack! Normally, it was the sort of high-end item he would have placed in his safe. But he'd absentmindedly taken it home on his birthday and found it again this morning.

This was the first good news he'd had all day.

"Risotto con funghi," Neil said, snapping his fingers.

"Watch your language!"

"No, you idiot. It means risotto with mushrooms. I picked up some fresh ones at the market this morning. Start chopping some onion and garlic. I'll get the oil."

Neil rushed over to the

backpack and retrieved the bottle, which he had carefully wrapped that morning in a clean white chef's shirt. He turned the fabric aside and smiled at the sight of the golden liquid. Carefully Neil turned the wax-covered cork, breaking the seal and releasing a pungent earthy aroma.

"Ambrosia," he said under his breath. "Perfect."

Neil placed a drop on the tip of his finger and touched it to his lip. It tasted even better than it smelled.

"I don't know what favor your friend owed you, but this stuff is magnificent," Neil said. A few drops in the risotto would act as a magic potion tying everything together.

"It'll turn the risotto from fantastic to Flambé-stic!" Larry chuckled.

For the next half hour Neil and Larry worked furiously. The fish arrived and Larry sliced it into a perfect fillet as Neil stirred the risotto. Neil stole a few glances through the window at Chili, who was sitting as still as a statue. "If we can get a good review from Chili, it won't matter what the local losers say about this place," Neil said as he added a final dash of cheese and butter to the simmering rice.

Neil brought the risotto into the dining room personally. Chili finally moved, sniffing the air, and making a few notes. Neil placed the dish before him. Chili took his fork and carefully lifted a small bite to his lips. He sniffed but didn't say a word. Neil had the distinct impression that Chili would prefer to examine and taste the dish alone. Neil said, *"Bon appétit"* and returned to the kitchen.

Larry looked up as Neil walked through the doors. "What did he say?"

"Nothing. But we have to keep moving. Fire the grill for the salmon. I'll make a quick maple syrup glaze. Run up to the roof and grab some mint from the herb garden."

Larry saluted and ran.

Neil delivered his *pommes de terre à la Flambé*, his signature dish, with a beet and onion salad. It was, he was sure, the exclamation point on a sentence written in all caps. Chili reacted with barely a comma.

Neil was rattled to see the risotto sitting, almost untouched, next to Chili's notebook. *Don't panic. Critics don't always finish the dish*, he told himself. *They just need to taste it to get the idea.* Still, leaving behind risotto with good-as-gold truffle oil? That was weird, and troubling. Neil was desperate to know what Chili had written in the book, but it was closed. Chili opened it again as Neil retreated into the kitchen.

Certainly Chili would finish the potatoes, Neil told himself. They were sublime. Even a jaded critic wouldn't say no to a plate full of the crisp, seasoned Neil Flambé specialty.

But when he returned a few minutes later, the majority of the potatoes were there, cooling on the dish next to the barely touched salad.

Neil began to say something but Chili abruptly held up his hand to silence him. Then Chili carefully flaked the salmon onto his fork and placed a small morsel in his mouth. He swallowed and then carefully placed the utensils back down on the linen tablecloth.

He sat for a long time, running his finger along his

mustache and occasionally making a low *hmmmm* sound.

Neil didn't move or say a word. He felt like a condemned prisoner, standing against a wall waiting for the sergeant at arms to yell "fire." Finally Chili opened his notebook with one more *hmmmm*, scribbled a few short words that Neil couldn't read, closed it, and stood up.

"Shocking," he said. "Worse zan I feared." He paused, shaking his head. "Much worse, I am afraid to say." He walked past Neil, shaking his head and seemingly lost in thought.

Neil's legs began to shake. His chest tightened. Dots floated before his eyes and his head swam. He took quick breaths through his nose. Disaster, absolute disaster . . . that was his life right now. He could ignore the musings of the local critics, but disappointing Jean-Claude Chili was another level of awesome bad, as Larry would say. Of course Larry also thought scallops were a kind of potato, so Neil didn't always go with what Larry said.

Things couldn't possibly get any worse.

Behind him, Neil heard Chili turn the handle of the door.

Neil sensed this was a crucial moment in his life. If he let Chili out that door without an explanation, without some kind of plea for another chance, he would be giving up on his future.

"Wait," Neil called out. "Chili, wait." He heard the door open.

He turned around to stop Chili, to try to offer some kind of explanation, even if he didn't have one. But the opening door wasn't letting Chili out, it was letting two more people in. One was Chief Inspector Sean Nakamura. The other was a severe woman Neil had never seen before.

"Nose, I mean Neil, this is Greta Carbo. She's with the City Health Department."

"And?" Neil said, with a growing sense of unease. "Why is she here? Is this about the restaurant across the street?"

"No, still no leads on that. She's here because, well, I'm afraid we have to shut you down—temporarily."

"What? Why?"

Nakamura pulled out his notebook and flipped it open. "There were four cases of severe food poisoning reported this weekend. The connection is that all four ate salmon here at Chez Flambé."

Silently, Carbo walked up to the front window and taped a CLOSED BY ORDER OF THE OFFICER OF HEALTH notice. Then she walked out. "I'll come back in a bit," Nakamura said, following her.

"Perhaps eet eez for zee best that this happens," Chili said, nodding solemnly.

As Neil watched Chili walk out the front door, a dump truck filled with sticky tar pulled up in front of the restaurant, followed by a bulldozer and steamroller.

A man in work clothes

walked up and opened the door a crack. "Just want to let all the people on the street know that we've got some street and sewer work to do for the next couple of weeks. Might be a bit noisy. Might smell a bit too." He gave a little wave and closed the door.

Larry came up beside Neil. "I have a me-shirt back home that says 'shoot me now.' Want me to go get it?"

"Yes," Neil said weakly.

Chapter Six

Something Smells

Neil watched as a few customers walked up to Chez Flambé, spied the notice from the health department, and quickly scurried away. *Just like rats from a sinking ship,* he thought. Looking past their fleeing backs, Neil could see the dark windows of Carrion staring blankly back at him. Two tiny spots of light seemed to glimmer for a second, staring back, but when Neil tried to get a closer look, they disappeared. Great. Sight was now joining taste and smell as senses he couldn't trust anymore.

Neil could hear Larry in the kitchen, doing his best to clean up the mess that the safe thieves had left behind. Neil felt he should probably go in and help him, but he just didn't have the energy.

Nakamura had walked through the kitchen and taken some notes. He'd even dusted for finger-prints but found nothing.

"I can't really come back with a full forensic team,"

Nakamura said. "The sad truth is that break-and-enters—"

"B-and-E's," Larry said.

"—yeah, B-and-E's happen all the time in this part of town, so we can't afford to investigate them all."

"That's how I keep meeting my rent payments," Larry joked.

"Ha, ha. Trust me. If I thought I could throw you in jail for a few years, I'd spring for a forensics team out of my own pocket. Anyway, Nose, that's all I can do right now. I've got to get back to the office and do some paperwork."

Nakamura braced for the high-decibel stream of abuse he was sure Neil was going to hurl his way. *Paperwork? After all I've done for you?*—something like that, anyway. But Neil just sat at his table in the dining room and nodded silently.

"Well, I'll keep looking into the place across the street," Nakamura said, hoping to at least get a grunt from Neil. Neil just nodded again.

"I think he means, 'Thanks, Nakamura.' He's just a little beaten up," Larry said finally, and let Nakamura out the back.

Neil had barely moved since. Did that symbol burned into the door have anything to do with all this? Where had he seen it before? He had a nagging feeling he'd seen something like it more than once. And what had gone wrong with his taste buds? Had he actually served rotten food? That would be unforgivable.

"Hey, Neil, check it out," Larry called from the kitchen. "You never opened the package your parents left for your birthday."

"Oh. Where is it?"

Larry walked out and handed him the package. "I just found it jammed against the back of the wall under the filing cabinet. It must have landed there after it flew off your desk the other day."

"Great. If it's from my mom and dad it's probably a get-well-soon card they got by mistake."

"Look, chef-boy. You are in some serious need of cheering up. Maybe it's a big wad of cash!" Larry smiled. Neil just shrugged his shoulders and put the package down on the brand-new linen tablecloth, hand-stitched in Ireland. He glanced at the new silverware he'd bought . . . splurged on, really. He'd even had "CF" ornately inscribed on each handle. He gently fingered one of the spoons. They were so expensive he could afford only one set per table. The CF, he thought, would also make them easier to identify if someone tried to walk off with a souvenir.

Maybe he could hock them now to cover the losses he was going to face. What was it his mother had said about a really good piece of silver? "You can always tell a good piece of silver by the mark. It tells you the maker, and the amount of silver they used. The bigger the number the better." Neil turned the spoon over in his fingers.

There was a tap at the door. Neil put down the spoon and looked up. It was Isabella Tortellini.

She gave a smile, and despite himself, Neil smiled back.

"I'll get it," Larry said, reemerging from the kitchen.

"It's okay," Neil said, standing. "I've got this one."

Larry saw Isabella and smiled. Then he saw Jones standing on the curb with his arms crossed and a scowl across his face. "I've never seen him look happier," Larry joked. "Which, come to think of it, is actually true."

Ever since Isabella had been kidnapped in Mexico City, Jones had hung around her like pesto on pasta—an incredibly frightening pesto. He wasn't a huge fan of the Flambés at the best of times . . . and he made clear to them, repeatedly, that only a heartfelt plea from Isabella had prevented him from breaking them both in two when they'd gotten back from Mexico.

Isabella gave Neil a huge hug, as Jones audibly cracked his knuckles and waited outside. Neil sat back down, keeping an eye on Jones. Isabella sat across from him.

"Neil, I am sorry we fought. Larry gave me a call and told me of the horrible day you have had."

"I also called the twins and told them not to bother coming in tomorrow," Larry said.

"Is there anything I can do?" Isabella said.

"Can you cook?" Neil moaned. "Or bribe the Health Department?"

"I eat. You cook." She frowned. "What happened to the cocky young Neil we all know and love?"

"Love?" Larry said. "I don't know what Neil you find lovable, but the cocky one keeps throwing ladles at me in the kitchen."

"Fine," Isabella said. "Then what happened to the cocky Neil that we admire?"

Neil didn't say anything. He wasn't sure what to say. Isabella reached across the table and laid a hand on Neil's. She spied the twine-covered package that Neil had left unopened.

"What is this?" she said, her eyes growing wide. Before Neil could say anything, Isabella had grabbed the package and slipped off the string. Neil watched with mild interest as she ripped the paper, exposing a leather-bound notebook.

"Oh, please. Not another antique book." Larry sighed. "Every time one of those shows up here, someone starts knocking off chefs."

"It is a very old book," she said, flipping the pages open. "It's in French. No, wait. Some is in French, some is in German . . . and there are other languages as well, even English. And there are some symbols and things written around the edges."

She slid the book across the table to Neil. One thing a love for French cuisine had given him was an aptitude for French. It was the one subject he wasn't failing so far at school. He flipped through the pages.

"It's a recipe book," he said. He sat up in his chair, suddenly interested. He greedily ran his fingers along the lines of ingredients and instruction.

"Wow," he said, letting out a low whistle. "My parents must have picked this up in an antique shop or something."

"What kind of recipe book?" Larry and Isabella said together.

Neil tapped his forehead. "Well, how do I explain this to you two so that you can grasp it . . . ?"

They groaned.

Neil continued. "These are some amazing . . . well, amazing recipes . . . possibly mind-blowing, actually, if they are right." Neil paused. He closed his eyes and seemed to be adding ingredients in his imagination. His fingers danced in the air, as if he were selecting and adding spices from an imaginary spice rack. "Wow," he said with chuckle. "I never thought of adding those two together. Simple, really . . . but magnificent."

Isabella and Larry exchanged glances. Neil Flambé admitting he had never thought of something to do with great food? This must be one heck of a recipe book. "Um, you wanna share some of your insights with the rest of the class . . . stupid as we are?" Larry said.

Neil closed his eyes and licked his lips, tasting the imaginary combination. "Amazing," he said, with another laugh. He quickly flipped the pages. "Look. It's a whole series of amazing recipes."

He turned the book around on the tabletop so that Larry and Isabella could see.

"They all use different ingredients. Lots of different and strange ingredients."

Larry ignored the recipes and examined the numbers in the margins. "They seem to be written by different people. Look. This first recipe has a date in the margin next to it. 1293? Wow."

Isabella nodded. "There are only two or three ingredients listed."

Neil smiled. "There's not even any pepper or salt in that recipe, yet it's . . . succulent." He flipped ahead. "This one even has some pineapple in the recipe, and it's for snails!"

"Yeah." Larry gagged. "Delicious. I can't wait to add that one onto the menu." He looked back at the notebook. "That gem is dated 1892."

Neil nodded. "These chefs, if those dates are right, are years ahead of their times."

Larry looked at the book again. "Hmmm. I'll take your word for it. There are also some notes and other dates and some names written in the book, but the handwriting is a little hard to read."

Isabella looked as well. "They just seem to be random words in French, Latin, Greek . . . and many symbols."

"Weird."

"It doesn't seem to have anything to do with the important stuff, the food," Neil said. "This chef, or the chefs, are geniuses. I wish I still had a restaurant open so I could try some of these recipes."

Just then the air conditioning unit kicked in, sending cool air through two carefully hidden vents in the ceiling over the kitchen door. It was state-of-the-art, timed to kick in just as the dining room started to feel a little warm from the first seating. There were five filters to keep the air as clean and as pure as possible.

Neil turned to Isabella and put his nose near her shawl. He sniffed.

"Excuse me?" Isabella said.

"What happened to your perfume?" Neil said.

"It's Chapultepec Chili and Chocolate, one of my new Aztec scents. Do you like it?"

"It smells like wet dog," Neil said.

Isabella pursed her lips and poked a finger in Neil's face. "You little *moccioso*."

"That means 'brat' in Italian," Larry whispered to Neil.

Isabella poked the finger at him with renewed menace. "Neil Flambé. I just watched you treat Angel like this. You can't speak to me that way. You may be a great chef but if you don't learn a lesson or two about *il tattoo*—"

"Tact," Larry translated, enjoying the show.

"*Sí*, if you don't find some tact, you are going to find yourself customerless and friendless."

Neil backed away with his palms in the air. "No, no, no. That's not what I meant. I mean that when you came in, I knew you were wearing a perfume and I knew it was chili based. I liked it . . . although the chocolate overtone needs a little tweaking."

Isabella took a step toward Neil and brandishing her finger like a sword.

"B-b-b-b-but," he stammered, "I just mean that as soon as the AC kicked in, it smelled different, less like chili and more like chihuahua."

"And? What of it?"

"Nothing, just that something changed. But it shouldn't have . . . unless. Larry. Quick, go shut off the AC!"

"Aye aye, Captain Cook." Larry ran into the basement. A few seconds later the AC shut down, and the cool flow of air stopped.

Neil ran over and opened the door and windows. "Let's wait a few minutes," Neil said.

As the fresh air poured into the room, Neil took a few deep sniffs through his nose. He shook his head in wonder. "Darn it," Neil said, but he began to smile. "That's it! That's the problem." He began to clap his hands. He was practically skipping around the room now. "What a relief!"

Larry, having come back up the stairs. tapped him on the shoulder. "Um, Neil, maybe you can let the rest of us in on the big relief?"

Neil stopped dancing and placed his hands on Larry's shoulders. "It's not me. The stupid AC unit was mucking up the air out here. That's why the critics didn't like the food. It wasn't me, it was the AC!"

"The AC?"

"Yes. It kicked in and changed the way Isabella smelled. Smell and taste are tied together. That's why my nose is more important than my taste buds when I cook. It must have altered the food I was serving." Neil felt a rush of relief pour over him. "I can't believe it was so simple. Oh, my goodness. I need to call those critics. I need to . . . celebrate . . . I need to cook. . . ."

Neil headed for the kitchen. "I'm feeling hungry. Let's eat. How about salmon?"

"But Neil, wait a minute," Larry said, considering. "Jean-Claude Chili ate way before that AC unit kicked in . . . and he hated your food."

Neil felt the doubt creeping back in, but he fought it. "I don't know what that was about. He never said he hated it. . . . He just said things were odd, or worse, or something. . . . Maybe I was rattled and made some mistakes. . . . NEVER MIND! I'll figure it out later." Neil desperately clung to the elation he was feeling, the conviction that he'd found the answer and it wasn't his fault.

"Okay, if you say so."

"Look! It's the AC. It has to be. It's emitting some kind of nasal blocker and that's warping the tastes. Smell and taste are intertwined. No one knows that better than me. No one."

"Well, how about the food poisoning?" Larry said.

"Would you please shut up!" Neil yelled.

"There a problem here?" Jones seethed. He'd now opened the door and was clutching the handle so tightly it seemed to creak under the stress of his grip.

Isabella put her hand on Neil's shoulder. "You may have solved part of the mystery," Isabella said. "Maybe only one part, but it is part. Be happy about that. Now work hard to solve the rest. We've been through worse." She gently fingered her short hair, cut by crazed Aztec kidnappers.

Neil slumped back in his chair, feeling overwhelmed by the number of questions. Why was life always like that? Every answer just led to more questions. That's why he preferred food to people. Food was much simpler.

Although even that was getting more complicated these days. He groaned.

Larry walked over to the vents. "So we should call in the company that made the AC and have them come and service the filter system."

"The twins were here when it was installed and the paperwork was in the safe," Neil said. "I don't even remember who we ordered it from."

"No problem . . . when I took the front of the panel off the AC unit, the company's name was written on the pipes inside."

"Why didn't you just flip the breaker?" Neil said, staring at his cousin.

"Why don't you just serve boiled potatoes? I was being creative!" Larry said. "Besides, it's on the same breaker as the coffee machine and, well, there's no way I'm shutting THAT off."

"Fine, give me the name of the company and I'll look it up." Neil flipped his phone open.

"It was DBC Systems. I think it stands for Danish Blizzard Cooling."

"What? Why?"

"Because that would be so cool! So to speak."

"Go get your coffee." Neil shook his head and began to type the name into his phone, and stopped. His head shot up. "Wait. Did you say DBC Systems?"

"Um, yeah, three letters. DBC. Why?"

Neil gritted his teeth, and slammed the phone down on the table.

"I should have guessed. Picón, you jerk. If you can hear me, I'll get you for this!"

Isabella, Jones, and Larry stared at Neil.

"Um, Neil, cuz, who are you talking to? I'm starting to think your eggs are getting a little scrambled, if you know what I mean."

Neil ignored Larry and started pacing the floor, waving his arms as he spoke out loud. "Picón. DBC. It's just like them. They have the resources, the technology. They've probably bugged the place too. Picón, I'll track you down and get you for this!"

"Um, still not following you, cousin."

"Neil, who is this Picón?" Isabella said.

Neil stopped and stared at the three confused-looking faces. He seemed shocked to find them still there. "Um, DBC. Larry said DBC. And it doesn't stand for Danish Blizzard Cooling or anything idiotic like that. DBC stands for evil."

"Um, Neil, I don't think evil has a *d*, *b*, or a *c* in it."

"Not literally!" Neil bellowed. "D, B, and C are the initials for . . . Deep Blue Cheese."

Chapter Seven

Deep Blue Cheese

Deep Blue Cheese hummed contentedly. Life was good. Deep Blue Cheese—DBC to his closest friends—didn't need sleep or food, just a chance to work and play and sometimes compose songs like the one he was humming now, a little ditty DBC liked to call "Happiness Is a Warm Bun—An Ode to John Lemon."

There was nothing DBC liked better than working and playing with food, with recipes. Just give DBC five ingredients and DBC could spit out an almost infinite number of possible combinations of succulent dishes, mathematically precise in their balance.

Sadly, DBC could never actually taste any of them. Not that DBC

would use the word "sadly." DBC didn't feel sadness in any way humans would understand. DBC was a computer—a superfast, superintelligent, supertalented computer. *Well, of course he is super,* his proud father would say. *He was programmed that way.*

A chewing noise came from behind the humming mix of DBC's transistors, wires, microprocessors and superconductors. The chewing noise was coming from a tiny man who was doing a little fine-tuning of DBC's circuitry. Stanley Picón was nibbling on some world-class truffle-infused goat cheese he'd picked up on a recent trip to Hungary while he poked around the main memory bank of his beloved creation. Nothing was out of line, so he gave a satisfied sigh, swallowed his cheese, and placed the protective panel back on.

He stood up and wiped his hands on his lab coat. Not that there was any dust on the floor of DBC's inner sanctum, as Stanley called it. But it was a nervous habit for Stanley, a man who was always nervous. Today, though, Stanley was feeling a certain sense of elation along with his nerves.

He was going to ruin that little punk, Neil Flambé. Just as Flambé had once inflicted ruin on him—on him and his beloved DBC, to be more precise.

Stanley's whole body shook with anger as he relived their humiliation. He ran to the fridge for more gourmet cheese. As he gobbled his gouda greedily, he felt his nerves calm, but the memories flooded back.

Stanley Picón was a computer genius, but a reluctant one. His true love was the kitchen. His parents had been great chefs on their Caribbean island home, and had even risen to the status of personal chefs to the island's dictator Fidel Castoroil.

One big problem with the job—they hated Castoroil with a passion. And one hot summer night they attempted to poison him with a pork sausage that was months past its "best before" date. He'd mistaken it for a cigar and lit it instead of eating it, immediately smelling the rot. The Picóns fled for their lives, and vowed never to let their son work in such a dangerous trade.

"You think cooking is all fun and games, but it is serious business," his father had told him as they made their perilous escape in a leaky boat, stowed away and cowering under the tarp. "You have other talents, better talents. Use them. Do not waste your life standing in front of a stove working for pennies."

There was no doubt that Stanley was technologically gifted. On the island, he had once assembled a calculator out of discarded car radio parts. In their new home in Miami he had access to more materials, and constructed a laptop computer when he was just twelve years old.

His parents had opened a seafood restaurant on the beach, and he programmed the laptop to cool down or heat up all the electronics in the kitchen, depending on what orders came in from the waitstaff. He'd even worked out an algorithm that could predict what a customer would order the second they walked in the door, based on a complex analysis of data such as age, weight, hair color, and how thick a wallet or purse they were carrying.

"Put your mind to something useful," his father told him, unimpressed. "I forbid you to waste your life in a kitchen." Then he'd disconnected the laptop and ordered Stanley out of the restaurant. Stanley had cried, but he had honored his father's wishes and applied his skills to more lucrative endeavors.

He'd gone on to design a program for the U.S. Army that could launch missiles five minutes before the President even knew he wanted to (he called it "preemptive prognostication"). Another Picón creation could keep tanks moving and firing shells even when there was no one left to fire or be fired on (he called that "postapocalyptic precision"), but somehow he still felt empty inside.

A few years later, his parents now departed for the great kitchen in the sky, Stanley struck on an idea so perfect that he'd practically exploded on the spot. The spot had been Madrid, specifically the outdoor patio at Carlos LaMancha's Café Molino. As Stanley sat eating breadsticks, Chef LaMancha had chased one of his sous-chefs out onto the terraced steps of the patio, throwing plates, knives, and finally a blender at the terrified young man.

The problem? The sous-chef had neglected to add three-quarters of a teaspoon of sea salt to the tarragon sauce for the chef's signature dish, Pancho Pasta. "You have ruined everything!" LaMancha had screamed as the unfortunate apprentice jumped over a railing and into the river that backed up to the patio.

Hmmmm, Stanley had thought, watching LaMancha throw a series of potted plants at the young man, who swam as fast as possible to the other side, successfully dodging the lethal ferns. *Perfection seems so elusive to humans, but why? Really it's just a matter of getting the recipe right.* It was like math. Recipes were like formulae. A chef needed only to add the right amount of A to the right amount of B, in combination with the constant C, taking into account variables D and E. It was so simple, and obvious. Why did chefs have so much trouble figuring it out?

That was the moment of his great idea—a way to take the human factor out of the equation . . . to guarantee the perfect meal each and every time. Stanley pulled one of his many pens out of his shirt pocket and began scribbling different configurations, formulae, and program parameters on a series of napkins.

By the time the police arrived to handcuff LaMancha and take him away, Stanley had a stack of napkins that formed the blueprint for his new mission in life—Deep Blue Cheese.

When he returned to the U.S., he told his bosses at the military that he was working on a computer that would help build an army that wouldn't need expensive rations. They had given him a blank check for the operation.

Within a year, Stanley had a prototype. He had programmed in the recipes from every possible cookbook. Would DBC be able to replicate them? Stanley took a deep breath and walked calmly up to the giant gleaming blue stack. He pressed the on button. A stream of lights buzzed and illuminated.

"Would you like to plate some game?" DBC said with a smooth electronic voice.

Stanley cried as if the computer had just said "Daddy." "Yes, Deep Blue Cheese," he said. "Please make me a venison and cheese omelet."

"Isn't that a tad simple?" DBC responded.

Stanley smiled. "Not at all. The French have a saying; 'There is no such thing as an adequate omelet.' It's either great or it stinks, and I'm expecting the best omelet ever made."

DBC retrieved the recipe, and processed two million possible variations in a millisecond. Then he sent out a series of instructions to the kitchen that Stanley had set up in the adjacent room. The stove fired up. A robotic hand held an omelet pan over the flame, warming it to a perfect temperature. In went exactly 8.3546789 grams of butter, and 26.98763554 milliliters of olive oil. In a stainless-steel bowl, DBC tossed in 37 grains of organic sea salt, two eggs weighing exactly 125.763 grams, 3 crushed peppercorns (minus 5.4 grains that DBC deemed unsuitable), and 18 milliliters of distilled water.

Then it was all cooked over a high flame, with a last-second addition of equally

accurate amounts of grated cheese, shaved venison, and fresh parsley, and served on a prewarmed plate.

The result exploded on Stanley's taste buds. DBC replicated the experience over and over again

Stanley happily patted his full belly and then his equally packed brain. DBC was ready. But ready for what? Stanley's personal goal was to change the future of cooking forever, but he knew his military bosses weren't going to accept that as an explanation for the millions they'd sunk into his top-secret project.

DBC would have a military application, of course. Stanley's idea was to use DBC as a kind of remote cook. DBC would stay in his bunker and send out cooking instructions to robot cooks in the field. Score one for nutrition. The troops would get better food, and better-fed troops would be better soldiers. Economically, it also meant the military could eliminate at least a thousand high-paying cook jobs . . . and the health care benefits that went with them.

To demonstrate that potential to the military brass, Stanley knew he'd need a wow factor—definite proof that DBC was not only nonhuman but was better than a human.

But which chef would be a worthy opponent? Stanley wanted to demonstrate that DBC could beat the best, so he was going to ask a famous superstar chef. Then the critical, warning voices of his parents came back to him.

You don't belong in a kitchen.

Cooking is not for you.

Stick to computers.

He considered. He couldn't risk failure. A robot

cook was already going to be a hard sell. Maybe he needed to put DBC through a warm-up battle first, like a prizefighter who faces a weaker opponent—a palooka. A fight to get in shape for the championship bout without really risking injury. By chance, he opened his copy of *Gastro Gourmet* magazine to a small article about a precocious boy chef named Neil Flambé.

"I believe that I have found my perfect palooka," he said with a smile. There was no way any kid could beat a supercomputer. Once DBC trounced this punk, they'd face someone really good, like Bobby Filet or Kit Coriander. That battle would take place in front of TV cameras at a huge press conference. This skirmish with the kid was strictly a private show to get Stanley's bosses onside.

"DBC. Can you find the home phone number for Neil Flambé?" Stanley said.

"Piece of cake, devil's food cake . . . ," DBC purred.

"Not only talented, but witty." Stanley chuckled. *Maybe I programmed him too well.*

Neil had shown up on the big day with a quizzical look on his face. He'd been asked to come for a cooking demonstration, and was being paid handsomely, but he was a little taken aback by the military escort from the Canadian border, and the odd layout of the kitchen. It was laid out in a large airplane hangar, with top military brass seated in folding chairs next to a table of three judges, whom Neil recognized as the hosts of the paramilitary cooking show *Rifles and Trifles*.

"Excuse me, Colonel Mustard," he said, turning to face the four-star general who was sitting in the front row.

"Why are there two cooking stations? And what is that big blue humming thing behind that stupid-looking stove?"

"That's a good question, civilian." The general looked at the large gleaming blue tower. It sat behind a stove that had robotic arms coming out of the top. The fingers on the arms were tapping impatiently. "Picón, what the heck is that thing? I hope it's some kind of robot soldier. That's what we're paying you for."

Stanley looked up from the table where he was laying out a full complement of fresh ingredients. He pushed his glasses back up on his nose. "I never promised a soldier, General. I promised to find a more efficient, economical, and, dare I say it, brilliant way of feeding our troops. This is the answer."

"What is it? Some kind of mobile vending machine?" the general growled.

Stanley coughed. "Um, no. Deep Blue Cheese is the computerized future of haute cuisine . . . and military meals. Wasn't it Napoleon who said an army marches on its stomach?"

"Yes." The general nodded. "But isn't Beef Wellington named after the guy who beat him?"

Stanley ignored this, partly because he wasn't quite sure what the general meant. Then he spied Neil Flambé, short and skinny, and could barely suppress a smirk. "Ah, I see the competition is here."

"Competition?" Neil said. "So that's what's going on, some kind of competition, like a duel?"

Stanley walked up to shake Neil's hand. "I am Stanley Picón. You could say I am DBC's . . . creator."

Neil kept his hands on the counter. "Seriously? You

really think 'fission chips' over there can beat a real chef?"

"After he beats you I guess we'll find a real chef and figure that out . . . kid," Picón said. He would live to regret that word.

Neil said nothing and calmly turned to his workstation, unsheathing his custom-made knives.

Stanley turned to the military brass. "Gentlemen, I ask your patience and perhaps your indulgence; I realize this is an unorthodox presentation. But I promise to show you something in the next few minutes that will save the military millions and make our soldiers better fighters."

The officers nodded their agreement. "But it had better be good," a colonel with a southern accent said. "We don't like surprises."

Stanley smiled.

"Let's get this over with. Three dishes. The best cook wins. Dish one, pesto risotto."

Neil immediately started cutting onions and garlic. DBC took a sensor reading of the air and added a tiny bit of salt and pepper to his own spice mixture. Stanley had already programmed the recipe into DBC's data banks, and he knew DBC was going to make the perfect dish.

What Stanley didn't count on was Neil's ability to tell what DBC was working on, and to make last-second adjustments of his own to compensate, like adding a cupful of diced squash to his mixture, adding a layer of subtle sweetness to combat the acidity of the wine and sundried tomato pesto.

It was a combination that was way off from the recipe, and shouldn't have worked, but somehow Neil had made it all blend together perfectly. On a hunch, Neil also chopped dozens of pungent cloves of garlic that he hadn't actually used in his dish. Neil didn't think DBC could smell, but he was pretty sure the computer was making adjustments based on what it saw Neil was using. So Neil kept the garlic on the counter right until it was time to eat, then dumped it all in the composter.

DBC fell for it, making a series of ill-advised adjustments such as adding more basil to the pesto. The last-second addition didn't cook thoroughly . . . and that threw the balance of flavors in the risotto completely off.

The judges were unanimous. Neil had made a far more complex, interesting, and tasty dish. "This makes no sense, Father," DBC said as Stanley leaned in close to

examine DBC's circuits, and to hide the beads of sweat that were forming on his forehead. "My dish was perfect. How could the judges have preferred his dish? There was so much garlic in it."

"Don't worry, DB. The next dish is a rib roast with roasted potatoes. There's no way that insignificant worm can mess with that. This time stick close to the recipe and don't fall for any of the boy's tricks." But again, Stanley's instincts had been wrong. This time the difference was the rosemary. Neil had used his sense of smell to determine that it wasn't as fresh as it should have been, so he didn't crush it, but cut it into tiny bits before rubbing it on the roast. He also used more than normal to extract more of the available flavor. DBC followed Stanley's order to stick to the recipe and made a very bland dish with bland rosemary.

By dessert it was over, and it was a rout. DBC began to overheat and was reduced to singing the theme to *The Galloping Gourmet* before finally blowing a memory card and shutting down. A small red "error" light was the only evidence that DBC was still present, as Neil handed his strawberry, rhubarb, and ginger flan to the judges.

Stanley had collapsed in absolute shock. He looked less animate than DBC.

"Hey, Picky, Pickle, Nose-picker . . . whatever your name is," Neil had said, strutting past the supine programmer. "Recipes are like paint-by-number sets. You can get an okay picture of a sunset on a lake, but there's no way you're going to paint the *Mona Lisa*." Then he'd walked over and stuck his tongue out at the computer, which let out a high-pitched whine and went completely black.

Neil packed up his knives, and without another word, sauntered out the door into a waiting jeep.

"Picón!" the four-star general bellowed. "Millions wasted and your glorified laptop can't cook better than a kid?"

Stanley stood up but still said nothing.

The general continued. "That's it. You are hereby reassigned to accounting! Now, roll that stack of junk out to the shooting range."

Stanley had done no such thing. He clenched his fists so hard his knuckles turned white and cracked. "This is not over," he hissed. He took DBC with him and told his coworkers in accounting that his beloved computer was a filing cabinet. Over the next few months Stanley secreted DBC part by part to his own home, hiding each little piece in the sole of his shoe. He tweaked the hardware and the software and just as meticulously plotted his revenge.

That revenge that was now close to coming together like that first perfect omelet.

Two small blue lights began to flash, reflecting off Stanley Picón's glasses.

"Yes, DBC, what is it?" Stanley asked.

"The boy chef has discovered us," DBC said, with what Stanley was certain was a tinge of disdain.

"Sooner than we had expected," Stanley said. "But not too soon."

"Perhaps it is time to call him?" DBC suggested. Stanley smiled. DBC sounded almost eager.

He gently placed his hand on the gleaming blue metal.

"Not yet, DBC. Not yet. But soon, very soon."

My sweet,

As I write this I do not know what will become of us.

But living with little I have learned to make the best of what is at hand. Life is like this.

This book has been a guide for me and let it guide you.

Your mother

Genevieve 1797   1836

Genevieve Flambé stirred the pot methodically and carefully. Ingredients such as pigeon and onion were precious commodities in prison. A broth this aromatic would certainly alert any guards and fellow prisoners to her skills. And fighting over food this good would lead to a bloody riot. It was times such as these that made her happy to be imprisoned alone, in a solitary cell on a small outcrop of rock in the North Atlantic.

A boat came from the mainland once a week, leaving her one moldy loaf of bread. She waited until the boats left the rock, then used the bread to lure a few unsuspecting pigeons

in between the bars of her cell window. Well, when she was lucky she lured pigeons. She made do with whatever bird showed up first.

Thank goodness her cousin Hortense had been able to smuggle her some spices and cooking utensils. That was thanks to a well-placed bribe. Wood had been harder to come by, and she'd even considered burning her precious notebook. But her one stroke of luck had been in discovering that much of the so-called stone in her prison wall was actually coal. She did sacrifice a few pages near the end of the book to start her first fire, then carefully protected her smoldering embers in a makeshift hole in the floor.

She hoped the Emperor was choking on his own lump of coal right now. She spat into the fire, sending a hiss of steam echoing off the walls.

The Emperor had discovered her in a remote café in the Alps when she was just fifteen. Her family was hiding out in the mountains for reasons they never quite explained to her. She'd become his favorite cook, and for good reason—she was brilliant.

The Emperor famously stated that an army marches on its stomach. It was one of the reasons he'd enlisted her to be his personal chef on what was to be his great campaign to take over Europe. It had started well. She'd even met and married a young soldier just before they set out from Paris.

Then, just as victory seemed certain, it turned around. Stomach cramps were the first indication that her cooking fortunes had turned for the worst. The Emperor was forever sticking his hand in his coat to calm the jumbles and rumbles that now followed each of her meals.

His mind began to wander. He made rash decisions on the battlefield. She'd served him her last meal as head chef of France off a silver dish the very morning of his final battle. He'd even boasted that winning the battle would be as easy as eating the wonderful breakfast. Sadly for France, he was right. The breakfast had inexplicably sent him to the bathroom with the runs, and sent his troops on the run. He wasn't so incapacitated that he couldn't issue a decree for her imprisonment on the spot.

Then he'd gone out and lost the battle, and her fate had been sealed.

Now, sitting in prison, she could feel her own stomach beginning to cramp, and she knew that in a few months she would not be alone in this cell. She would need to be strong. She forced herself to swallow a large bowlful of the broth.

"Hmm," she said to her unborn child. "Not bad at all, my sweet. Perhaps there is hope for us after all."

Chapter Eight

Pigeons and Pine

Neil looked at the array of odd ingredients he'd set out on the counter. It had taken him a while to track down some of the more esoteric herbs and spices (especially Finnish Pine tree bark—who had ever heard of such a thing?) but since the restaurant was still closed down, he had the whole day free to scour everything from the shops in Chinatown to the shady spice vendors he knew who hung out under the Lion's Gate Bridge.

He was going to get to the heart of this strange recipe book, starting with recipe number one. *Mouette cuit á la vapeur, en alglues*—seagull steamed in seaweed with spices.

"Seagull? Bagging one of those in a park might get you thrown in jail for animal cruelty," Larry said.

"The book says seagull has a fishy flavor, not a poultry flavor, so cod should work," Neil said. He flipped to the next photocopied page from the book. He and Larry had decided it would be safer to keep the original away from real food. So far Neil had photocopied and translated about half the recipes. Larry had the original with him on the far counter and was sitting on a stool poring over the pages.

"So seagull is the one food that doesn't actually taste like chicken?" Larry said, not taking his eyes off the book.

"Ha, ha. Apparently. Now, let's see. I wrap the fillet in a specific kind of seaweed— it's called Limu Kala—tough to track down here in Vancouver."

"Sounds . . . delicious," Larry gagged.

Neil carefully spread the seaweed out on a cutting board. "Then adding just a few herbs and poaching it slowly over boiling seawater should add both a silkier texture and richer flavor. Hmm, amazing technique. I can't wait to see how it turns out." Neil carefully tied rosemary, sage, thyme, and parsley together and slid them into the seaweed with the slightly scored fish. Then he tied it all up with more seaweed as string.

"Uh, yeah, whatever you say. You know I don't like fish, even cod," Larry said, flipping between a series of dictionaries and the book itself. Larry let Neil worry about the recipes. Larry was busy looking at the scribbles and notes in the margins of the book. So far he'd been able to decipher some of the notes, and names featured

prominently. "Pierre comes up a lot early on," he said, "but there are as many symbols as there are words. And there are big empty gaps between them. . . . Weird."

"Uh, yeah, whatever you say, cuz. You know I don't like cod, I mean, codes . . . just coffee," Neil said, doing his best Larry imitation.

"Ha, ha, ha."

"Codes are too much like math homework."

"You might want to take more of an interest. They do seem to show up in your life an awful lot."

"Who was the moron who thought DBC stood for 'Danish Blizzard Cooling'? Nice code cracking, genius."

"Fine, cuz, you figured out that one. So far you're one for one hundred."

The water began to boil and Neil carefully placed a bamboo steamer on the top of the pot. "Now that we've cut off DBC's gas attack I have to focus on getting this restaurant back in the good books."

The DBC air-conditioning unit lay in pieces on the basement floor, dismantled by Neil and Larry in an effort to find the source of the "nose pollution," as Larry called it.

Ripping out the circuit board had revealed a series of canisters that fed into the ducting. "I told you it was sabotage!" Neil had exclaimed with a mixture of anger and elation. Isabella and Jones had agreed to take the canisters back to her lab to see whether they were chemical blocking agents or dangerous gases. "You should really let Nakamura test them at the police lab," Isabella said.

"The last thing Nakamura said to me was 'you're closed for a week.'"

"Even your friends seem to be turning against you," Larry had said. He'd meant it as a joke, but something in Neil's lack of a reaction showed it hit a little too close to home.

Neil was starting to wonder who was really trustworthy. Angel hadn't called since the cake incident. He should have been used to Neil's temper by now. Nakamura didn't seem to be doing much to help find his safe. Jean-Claude Chili had arrived unannounced, ripped into Neil's cooking, and then disappeared. And the contractor he'd hired to do the high-tech work on Chez Flambé had installed an AC unit that was built by a crazy supercomputer.

"There was a kind of genius involved in DBC's plan," Neil said, smelling the whisper of steam that escaped the tight weave of the bamboo. "The canisters only fed the ductwork that went into the dining room. The dishes tasted perfect to me in the kitchen, but when they arrived out there, the gas—or whatever it was—changed the molecular structure of the air."

"Wouldn't you notice the change the instant you set foot in the dining room?"

"It would only kick in when the AC kicked in, which was after I was settled in the kitchen for the night. The AC always shut off before service was over, so by the time I was able to go into the dining room—"

"For your evening ego boost."

"—to chat up the customers and boost the tips that the twins graciously share with you. . . ."

Larry grinned. "That's what I meant."

"By then the gas had dissipated. Remember, I only noticed the gas yesterday because it altered a smell that I already recognized, Isabella's perfume."

"You must smell her a lot." Larry dodged the garlic clove that Neil whipped at his head and kept his eye on the book. "You better improve your aim, you might need to bean somebody with a garlic clove some day."

"It was a lucky duck by you," Neil said.

"Lucky duck, ha, ha." Larry smiled, relieved Neil wasn't too down to bicker.

Neil continued. "You know . . . it was lucky, in a way, that the food critics showed up that first night. Customers with normal palates might have noticed something strange about the food, but they would keep eating. The critics were more discerning and sent the dishes back. That's what got me looking for a problem. Of course the makeup and glue they were wearing distracted me from noticing the gas."

Larry gave a groan and sat up. "Time for a coffee break, and a walk."

Neil lifted the lid off the steamer and carefully

extracted the glossy green seaweed. "This dish smells sublime!" he said excitedly.

"I don't mean to burst your borscht, cousin," Larry said, standing up and stretching his legs, "but while the AC-DBC thing might explain the critics' reaction to the food, I ask again—how, exactly, does this explain the food poisoning and Chili's reaction?"

"I thought you were going for a walk," Neil said, frowning.

"Not an answer," Larry said.

Neil seemed more interested in the dish. "I don't know. DBC must have remotely triggered some gas release when he sensed I was serving food."

"He sensed?"

"Would you please leave me alone? I'll figure out how it all fits together later."

Larry shrugged. "Okay. I might be a while. I need to give the old eyeballs a bit of a rest."

Neil waved his hand in Larry's direction as his cousin left, keeping his attention on the fish. Neil unwrapped the seaweed and then flaked a sliver of the bright white fish onto the blade of his knife. He held the blade up to his nose, closed his eyes and took a deep sniff. "Oh, my . . . ," he said. He carefully picked the fish off the blade with his fingers and placed it on the end of his tongue. Then he took a small bite. "Oh, my . . . my . . . my," he said as the fish broke apart, releasing its complex aroma, texture, and flavors.

It was amazing and even better than Neil had imagined. Somehow the chef in the book had taken the simplest of ingredients and combined them in such a way that together they equaled FAR more than their parts. The key was the saltiness of the steam itself, mixed with the slightly sweet tang of the seaweed, sealing the moisture in the flesh while at the same time subtly seasoning the dish. But why so simple a recipe? Why not add just a little pepper, or garlic, or even a splash of wine?

Neil quickly tried the dish with each of these variations and found that, while the additions created a different and equally delicious end result, none greatly improved on the original. The foundation was the key.

By the time Larry came back, much later, sipping from his coffee mug, Neil had covered every bit of counter space with dishes from the recipe book and his own variations.

Larry whistled. "Whoa, you've been busy."

Neil nodded. "These recipes were all written by master chefs . . . geniuses," Neil said in an awestruck voice, wiping his forehead with a towel. His eyes were wide open.

"How do you mean?" Larry asked, staying a few feet away. "And please wipe that nutty look off your face before you answer, because you're kind of creeping me out a bit."

Neil pointed at the dishes. "I've followed the first five recipes in the book. They are incredibly . . . basic. Not simple, but basic. There's barely more than a few ingredients and some strange choices for meat and vegetables. Things like rock pigeon, seagull, raccoon, seal, narwhal . . . stuff you wouldn't find in a normal kitchen."

"So they were experimenting with weird foods?"

"Possibly. But chefs, if they are experimenting, would normally pull out all the stops."

"Meaning?"

"If they had had access to all the ingredients possible, they'd use them. That's what chefs do. They don't cook with less unless they *have* to—and any chef this talented must have been chef to a king. They'd have used complicated techniques or elaborate spices, or even specialized pans or ovens to keep these meats from either breaking down into mush or ending up like rubber." Neil started to quickly pace up and down the floor.

"You've been doing that a lot lately. You're going to wear a groove in the floor," Larry said, keeping his distance.

Neil kept pacing. "So the answer is that they had to make do with what they had."

"You think they were forced to cook these things?"

Neil stopped. "Forced? I don't know. I think, for whatever reason, they didn't have a lot of options. Look at the seagull recipe." Neil walked up to the dish and stared at it like a miner who'd found a giant nugget of gold in a mud puddle. "It's beautiful. The chef came up with a specific technique and combination of spices that shouldn't have worked but did . . . and does."

"Necessity is the mother of convection."

"The amazing thing is that, even when I added variations to the foundation—richer spices, better broths, different herbs—I barely improved the dish at all." Now Neil let out a low whistle. "Wow."

Larry was shocked. "I've never heard you sound so

blown away by someone else's cooking. Yours, yes, but another chef's? Neil, did you hit your head?"

Neil waved him off. "Don't be an idiot."

"But isn't this like the peasant food Angel's always talking about—simple, fresh ingredients, that sort of thing?"

"Not exactly. These recipes don't even include the ingredients most peasants have. Look at this recipe for vulture tortiere . . . there's no pastry!

"Where did you get vulture meat?"

"THAT'S NOT THE POINT! Look, the recipe says, 'Use the inner bark of one white pine tree to form a crust.' The bark softens with the fat from the meat. It becomes edible . . . and it's delicious!" Neil held his arms wide and stared at Larry.

"Ta-da! You look like a magician who just pulled a rabbit out of his hat."

"If I had, it would be cooked perfectly."

"Well, this all sounds sort of like alchemy," Larry said.

"Al who?" Neil said.

"Not who, what. You call *me* an idiot? You really should do your history homework."

Neil growled and fingered a clove of garlic like a baseball.

Larry continued. "Alchemy was a big deal for philosophers in the middle ages, a quest, really. They were all searching for some secret that

88

would turn really mundane things—like lead, for example—into gold."

Neil snapped his fingers, letting the garlic drop to the countertop. "Maybe that's it. This is like a food alchemist's notebook? Turning seagull or rock pigeon or tree bark into delicacies?"

"Exactly."

Neil tapped his lips. "So maybe they were on a quest to find perfect recipes. But still, why such basic ingredients?"

"Maybe that's explained in the notes," Larry suggested with a yawn. "I'll get back to work. But first I'll get the coffeemaker warmed up again." He reached for the plug, always just a few inches from wherever he was working. "Hey, where's the book?"

Neil looked around in a panic. He hadn't made copies of the last few pages of recipes. "I must have moved it when I was plating all the dishes."

They quickly lifted the plates, and searched under the pots and pans Neil had left strewn all over the counters, tables, and floor.

"Oh, no," Larry said, spying something brown floating in a pot of water in the sink. He leaped over and pulled out the soaking wet book.

"It's ruined!" Neil yelled. "You're such an idiot!"

"Wait, *I'm* an idiot?"

"You left the book out. You knew I was cooking. You know I use all the counters." Neil started hyperventilating.

"Hold on, Neil. Get a grip," Larry said as calmly as possible. "You've really got to stop getting so wound up."

Neil grabbed at his hair and slid down the side of the

stainless-steel counter until he was sitting on the floor. "Everyone is out to get me! Everyone is trying to ruin me, including you!" Neil grabbed at his hair so hard a few chunks came loose in between his fingers.

Larry had seen Neil in extremely stressful situations before—solving murders, trying to save Isabella, feeding a room full of Hollywood stars and their pets—but he'd never seen him lose it like this. He got on his knees and put a hand on Neil's shaking shoulder.

"Look. Neil. The book . . . the book isn't ruined. See, it's made from parchment and leather. It'll be fine. I'll just open it up and we'll let it air out."

Larry flipped the book open and pointed at the page. "See, it's all fi—" He gasped, staring at the page. Where there had been empty spaces on the dry surface, there now appeared dozens of words and symbols.

He could clearly see the symbol of a cross in a circle, and over and over again the letter *F* and the name Valette.

"I see you found the book." The words came from a deep voice in the back doorway.

Larry and Neil turned their heads and saw Angel Jícama staring back at them.

Chapter Nine

Explosive News

It doesn't appear to be an invisible ink," Angel said, looking over Larry's shoulder. "It's imprinted, or maybe carved, right into the parchment. When the book gets wet, the surrounding material swells up, revealing the letters."

"And symbols," Larry said. "Someone wanted to hide something." As the pages had dried up, the mysterious symbols had began to disappear. He and Angel hurriedly wrote them down on Neil's photocopies, as Angel tried to explain what was going on.

"I have no idea what's going on," he said.

"Didn't you leave me this book?" Neil said. He was still crouched on the floor, rocking back and forth, holding his knees.

Angel nodded. "I was told to."

"By . . . ?"

"That's a good question. It is a very complicated story," Angel said, pursing his lips.

"Try me." Neil was feeling agitated, and it showed.

He had felt stress before, but the past few days were worse than anything he'd felt before. Was he going crazy? His own behavior suggested "yes." With his restaurant closed down, interest accumulating on his growing debt . . . Neil Flambé goes out in search of expensive rare meats and spices? That was a little nuts, for sure. Or was the rest of the world going crazy? Now the one person he trusted more than anyone else had been keeping secrets from him . . . that were about him?

Angel took a breath and continued. "Not long after I first met you, I received a strange package. There was no indication of who had sent it. It was just left on my kitchen counter."

"In your apartment?" Neil asked, raising his eyebrows.

"Yes. And I was home at the time. It was very strange."

"You didn't smell a thing?" Neil said, suspicious.

Angel shook his head. "Inside the box were a letter and this book. The letter asked me to keep an eye out for you. Of course I found this odd, but since I was already doing so, I merely accepted it as the advice of someone who shared my concerns. It then instructed me to give you the book on your fifteenth birthday."

"You weren't tempted to open the package yourself?" Larry asked.

"The note said I was to keep it safe."

"So you left it on the counter without telling me?"

Angel looked confused. "I gave it to your father."

"What? Why?"

"After you criticized my cake icing, I'm afraid I was a little angry, and left before giving it to you. I soon calmed down but when I came back to the restaurant, you didn't seem in any mood to see me."

"Or anyone else," Larry added.

"I saw your father coming in to see you and he promised me that he would make sure you received it. I gave it to him at the front door. I assumed it was a safe delivery."

Neil gave a hollow laugh. This was one more example of the world's craziness. His parents are given an antique recipe book, containing some of the greatest recipes the world has ever seen, and his dad leaves it where anyone could take it or lose it. "This is why I don't trust anybody but me," he mumbled.

"I do need to talk to you about that icing," Angel said.

"Let me guess," Neil said. "When you got home, it tasted fine."

Angel nodded. "How did you know?"

"Deep Blue Cheese."

"I didn't use any cheese. It was a butter-based icing."

"No, Deep Blue Cheese is a computer. It rigged the air conditioning."

"A computer rigged your air-conditioning unit?"

Neil nodded. "I beat DBC in a duel. I am guessing it was time for his revenge. Anyway, it wasn't your icing that was the problem."

Angel nodded. "Okay."

"And therefore, Angel, I'm sorry I was so rude to you," Larry said in his Neil voice.

Neil scowled at his cousin. "Isn't it time for your coffee break?"

Larry smiled and tapped his full coffee mug. "As usual, way ahead of you."

"Only when it comes to coffee," Neil said sadly. "So why are you here now, Angel? Was it just to tell me about the icing?"

"In that package, along with the note and the book, there was a card with a phone number. It told me to call in case you faced an extreme challenge after turning fifteen. I called that number on your birthday."

"Didn't take chef-boy long to get in trouble, did it?" Larry said.

"Me being framed for serial chef murders wasn't trouble? Getting whacked in the head by a crazy Aztec warrior wasn't trouble?" Neil said, incredulous. "Larry and Isabella almost getting killed wasn't trouble?!"

"The note said to call after you turned fifteen. Besides, I knew 'extreme challenge' would refer only to your deepest fears."

Neil felt a chill down his spine. He wasn't sure why but something about Angel's seriousness made 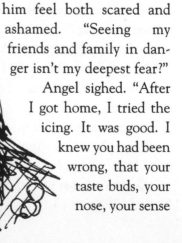 him feel both scared and ashamed. "Seeing my friends and family in danger isn't my deepest fear?"

Angel sighed. "After I got home, I tried the icing. It was good. I knew you had been wrong, that your taste buds, your nose, your sense of food was off. I knew that was the kind of trouble the note meant, the kind that would truly shake you to the center of your existence."

Larry shook his head in mock disgust. "Thanks, cousin. Isabella and I are less important than beef tenderloin. Nice, really nice . . . "

Neil wanted to protest, to say that nothing was worse than seeing your friends and loved ones in danger, but part of him knew that Angel was right. Having to face the idea that his cooking was no good, that he had lost his touch in the kitchen, was the toughest challenge he'd ever faced.

Angel smiled gently. "It's your nature, Neil. You want to be great. You love your friends, but cooking is who YOU are. Don't feel ashamed, just don't let it take over everything else."

"Who answered the call?" Neil said, avoiding Angel's gaze.

"No one. It was an answering machine."

"Was there a message?" Larry asked.

"Yes. It was a woman's voice, and it said 'If you are calling, it means that the curse has returned. Please tell me everything you know.' I said I knew you were having a crisis in your cooking and that I could not explain why."

Neil stood up. "Curse? How do you know who was on the other end of that phone call? How do you know it wasn't some enemy who was just waiting to be tipped off?"

"Tipped off to what?" Larry asked.

Angel stroked his beard. "I worried about this as well,

but I trusted my instincts. The person who left that number had asked me to call if you were in trouble. It was someone who was a friend, someone who wanted to help."

"And someone who predicted I'd be in trouble on my fifteenth birthday? Or wanted to cause trouble and then wanted to know if he or she, or IT, had been successful? Someone like a crazy computer programmer?"

"Perhaps I had been in such a hurry to find someone to help you that I was not as careful as I could have been. I tried to call back a few minutes later."

"Let me guess, another message?"

"No. The phone line had been disconnected."

Neil rubbed his hand across his temple. He was confused. Panic was rising up in him again. "We need to find out where DBC is. I need to find him to prove to everyone that it's not me that's the problem. It's a setup. It's not ME. And if DBC was behind that number, behind the book . . . then why?"

Just then the restaurant phone rang.

Neil walked over to the podium and looked at the Caller ID: "Unknown Number."

Neil picked up the phone without saying a word.

"Hello, Neil," said the voice. "It's Stanley Picón here. Perhaps you remember me."

Neil growled.

"I'll take that as a yes. I have a proposition for you, little boy."

"Let me guess—a rematch."

"Of course! But what a rematch. This one will be a winner-takes-all duel pitting your puny talents against my superior beloved, Deep Blue Cheese."

"Never, you weasel. The police will be on to you soon, once I find out what's in those canisters."

"Let me finish, you impetuous little jerk," Picón blurted. Then he coughed and resumed his calm tone. "You are going to be broke, out of business, and out of options in a matter of days. There is no money coming in, no money going out to your contractors. I believe you still owe DBC Incorporated Contracting about $25,652—if my calculations are correct, and they always are."

"*You* were the contractor we hired?"

"Just a subcontractor, specially hired to install the air-conditioning unit and the fans in the kitchen. . . ."

"And the hidden cameras and the microphones, I assume?"

"Only one of those, a combo camera and microphone in fact. Luckily I no longer have any need to spy on you. It's in the doorbell above the entrance."

Neil grabbed a steak knife from the place setting and expertly threw it. The doorbell fizzled and popped.

"Tsk, tsk. That was one of my favorite little gadgets," Stanley said. "I thought you could send it back. That will make it all the more pleasurable when DBC serves you your own head on a platter."

"I said I'm not interested."

"I am offering you one hundred thousand dollars, if you win. That is more than enough to keep you afloat, at least until you finally melt down under the weight of your ego. It doesn't match your talent, you know."

"And if you win?"

"*When* we win, you promise to never cook, to never lift so much as a teaspoon, ever again."

Neil felt sick to his stomach. As much as part of him wanted to destroy Stanley and DBC, part of him was still rattled—could he win?—and no part of him could face the prospect of never cooking again. "No. Not interested. Go back to your stupid bunker and bake your head."

"Ooooh, perhaps I should point out one more thing. You mentioned the canisters. I don't know how you'll ever find out what's inside. They are rigged to explode if anyone tries to open them up, unless DBC sends out a special signal to disable the trigger mechanism."

"WHAT!!!!" Neil screamed into the phone. "Isabella!"

"Ah, you gave them to your girlfriend—maybe your ex-girlfriend by now. And don't hang up on me to phone and warn her. If you do, DBC will send out a different signal, to make them blow up right away." He chuckled.

"I'll find you, Picón. I'll find you and that computer and I'll feed its circuits to you in a pie!"

"Agree to the duel and I'll make sure DBC protects your precious Isabella Tortellini. Oh wait, I can see through the camera I installed in the canister that she and a very large man—Jones, isn't it?—are about to hook up the first bit of gas to a release valve. Tsk, tsk. That's not a good idea."

"I AGREE, I AGREE, I AGREE!" Neil yelled.

Stanley sighed. "I knew you would. Wednesday evening at eight. I'll let you know the time and place at seven fifty-nine, so there's no time to warn your friend Nakamura."

"How am I going to get there in a minute?" Neil growled. "Wait—you own that restaurant across the way!"

Stanley hesitated. He must have put the phone against his chest because he said something that was too muffled for Neil to make out. Then Picón spoke into the phone again. "DBC says he doesn't know what idiot would open a restaurant in such a dumpy part of town, besides you."

"Keep insulting me, Picón. It will make beating you and that oversized laptop a pleasure."

"Be at your restaurant alone. Bring the ingredients for one dish, enough for two chefs. We'll provide the ingredients for the other dish . . . and the judges."

"I look forward to it!" Neil lied.

"And if you try to back out, we'll contact the banks, demanding payment . . . and you'll lose everything."

There was a click, and Stanley was gone. Neil's bravado disappeared and he whipped out his cell phone and dialed Isabella.

"Don't touch those canisters!" he blurted out as soon as she answered. The only response was the sound of an explosion, and then the line went dead.

Neil swooned and fell to the floor.

Basil J. Herrington II ran as quickly as he could around the corner of the crumbling tenement he now called home. He threw himself headlong into the shadows and stopped, hugging the wall. He strained to hear the sound of pursuing footsteps over his own labored breathing. He took a deep breath and slipped a small knife out of his pocket and readied himself to jump. But there were no footsteps, just the soft incessant patter of Liverpool drizzle in September.

Basil took a deep breath and relaxed a little. He pulled out the notice that had been pasted on the front door of his clandestine restaurant. Droplets of rain pelted the paper. He'd been selling covert gourmet meals for the city's elite out of a nearby warehouse for months. Then this evening, he'd arrived under a gloomy sky to prep his selections of eels and sturgeon, and seen the notice attached to his door with a spike. He'd pulled the notice down and bolted in a panic.

The cross and circle that had been painted on the paper left no doubt. They had found him, and they had come for him just as they had come for him in Paris. Of course, back then he was the marvel of the French bourgeoisie and their salons—the teenage boy who could amaze even the great Escoffier with his ability to cook anything with precision and perfection.

His name then had been Guillaume Flambé, and that name had been synonymous with the highest gastronomic quality. He knew there'd been a curse on his family. It had become a legend in the culinary circles of France, whispered in the kitchens of the great schools. But he also knew why the curse had been laid, and who had laid it. He'd broken the code of the notebook and discovered the truth hidden in the amazing recipes.

He'd taken the bold step of placing an ad in *Le Figaro* declaring that the long-rumored curse had been broken by the greatest of the Flambé family line. There was never a question of Guillaume's ego or his talent. But in retrospect he had to admit that the ad had been a mistake.

Instead of scaring the enemy into leaving the Flambés alone, the ad had lured them out of the shadows. One night, they confronted him head-on in his kitchen. He shuddered at the memory of how they had battled, leaving an entire city block in flames. In the end, his name was synonymous with death.

Guillaume had gone underground, but they'd found him again. He needed to do something more drastic. He left hidden clues behind in case anyone else tried to crack the code—strange carvings, notes tucked into recipe books. Then he faked his own death.

He fled across the Channel, changed his name, married, raised three children, and struggled to make it as a chef—all without raising attention, attention that would bring his past, his family's past, crashing down on him. He'd moved his restaurant from city to city, always underground, only accepting customers with references, never publicizing the menu, never letting the customers and chef meet. But somehow word got out. Now what?

He peered out of the gloom as the drizzle continued to fall, creating ghostly halos around the gaslight lamps. He was alone. He kept to the shadows as he sidled down the wall to the barred window of his basement apartment.

His wife and children were sitting at the dinner table. He tapped on the window. His wife, shocked, hurried over and slid the glass aside.

"Basil, what is it? Why do you look so frightened?"

"Hurry, pack up everything we have of value. I'll explain later."

His wife, Isobel, nodded and quickly ran to get the children. They had lived like gypsies for so long, but something in Basil's eyes was different this time.

Basil knew it would take only a few minutes, then they would resume their life on the run. He sighed. Then he heard the sound he dreaded, as frightening as any thunder or cannon fire—a slow, steady series of steps on the cobblestone. No one walked down the alleyways in this wretched part of town without a purpose, and Basil knew suddenly, without any doubt, that whoever was taking those steps was coming to kill him.

The footsteps moved slowly, inevitably closer. Soon the killer would turn the corner and know where he lived. Basil pulled out his notebook, the one possession that never left his body, and ran his finger over the words that were hidden inside. Isobel continued to assemble the household. Basil knew there was a boat leaving shortly for America. He reached into his pocket and pulled out all the money he had and slid it in between the final pages. He quickly scribbled a note on the last page, and dropped the notebook and money through the window.

Then he stood up straight and yelled to the

faceless pursuer, "I know you have come for me!" He turned and ran and prayed he could buy his family enough time to escape.

The next morning, sitting on the stern of the HMS *Stilton*, Isobel's tears wetted the last page of the notebook. Her beloved Basil had written: "Farewell, my love. You must run to America and start a new life. Hide, protect yourself and the children. . . . Change your name."

She tore out the page and held it to her chest.

The children, oblivious to the danger suggested in the words, played on the deck as a soft rain began to fall. Herrington had been her name for years now; what new name should she choose?

She unfurled the note.

Her tears and the rain fell on the paper, illuminating the name Flambé.

Chapter Ten

Hot Buns Crossed

Larry opened the kitchen doors a crack and checked on his cousin. Neil was asleep on the dining room floor, absolutely exhausted. Larry had covered him with a blanket. Neil was snoring away, but would periodically call out in his sleep. Sometimes it was "Picón, I'll get you!" Other times it was "I can't cook anymore. Why are you doing this to me?" but more often it was "Isabella!" or "NOOOOO!!!"

Larry allowed the doors to swing silently closed.

"That idiot actually thought I don't know what a booby trap looks like?" Jones scoffed, leaning on the counter, sipping the coffee Larry had made him.

"Hey, don't lean too hard on that counter, Mount Rushmore, we don't need any dents."

"How would you like one in your forehead?" Jones said, standing up.

"It's a good thing he can't read my shirt," Larry muttered to Isabella, who was sitting on a stool near the door, watching Neil through one of the round windows. "It says 'Only little people act big' or maybe it's 'brawny=stupid.' I can't remember." Larry grabbed his collar and peeked down the front of his shirt. "Second one."

Isabella didn't laugh. "Poor Neil," she said softly. "He is under such pressure. Being a chef is not an easy life."

Larry wanted to say *Yeah, and Neil makes it sooooo much easier*, but decided to keep that to himself for now. *Hey, that's kind of like a mental me-shirt. Only I know what I thought*, he thought. He turned his attention back to Jones.

"So why did the phone explode, then?"

"I had set the canisters out in the field behind the lab and attached the valve to let the gas out. I needed a timer trigger to open the valve after we got a safe distance away. Isabella needed a new phone. So I set the phone alarm."

"Neil called just as the timer went off?"

"Well . . ." Jones actually looked a little sheepish—or, Larry thought, more like a wolf in sheepish clothing. "That was an accident. I thought I'd blocked incoming calls. I guess I'd actually turned on the auto-answer function. Luckily Isabella and I were already behind the blast screen."

"Wait, you have a blast screen at a perfume factory?"

"Anybody ever tell you that you ask a lot of questions?"

"Too many?"

"Too many." Jones scowled and somehow sipped his coffee menacingly.

"You are the only man I know who can bruise coffee with his lips." Larry shuddered. Jones stood up. "I'm going to get back to work now," Larry said. He hurried over and opened the door to the office.

Angel was sitting behind the desk, looking at the recipes Neil had copied. "Neil's right. These are unique. If he'll let me, I would love to try them myself sometime."

"Yeah, seagull's a real treat." Larry gagged.

"How is our Neil?"

"Sleeping. After I told him Isabella was okay, he collapsed again. I don't think he's slept very much lately."

"I suspect that's always true," Angel said.

Larry nodded and pointed back to the book. "Do you see what I mean about that cross-and-circle thing?"

Angel nodded. He had gone out the back door to look at the symbol burned into the door. "It's the same as the one in the recipe book. It's not a symbol that I've seen before."

"But you said it was kind of familiar. Neil said the same thing."

"It's similar to the crest for Le Cordon Bleu."

"The cooking school?"

"Yes."

Larry thought for a moment. "Maybe it's Deep Blue Cheese making some kind of joke. Blue Cheese— Cordon Bleu. Of course that joke . . . bytes." Larry made air quotes.

Angel didn't laugh.

"That's bytes with a y," Larry explained.

"Yes. I got that."

"You didn't laugh."

"No. I didn't. But you're right. It could be Deep Blue Cheese, or Picón, using the symbol as a kind of signature of sorts. Was the symbol anywhere on the air conditioner?"

"Nope. And we tore that sucker completely apart. Neil almost cried. A new one is gonna cost thousands."

"Hmm. If they used it as a signature, you'd assume it would be somewhere on the unit. So that adds some doubt. Also, this isn't the Cordon Bleu crest, it's only *like* the crest."

Larry looked at the book. "Pierre was the first one to scratch it in . . . next to the date 1287. Did they even have cooking schools back then?"

"It's not as crazy as you might think. Le Cordon Bleu wasn't a cooking school until recently, but it can trace its history back to the late Middle Ages. It was originally a group of knights, known for their cooking, huge dinners, and amazing feats."

"So is this the symbol for those knights?"

"Not exactly. They shared the crest the school still uses today. And I said *late* Middle Ages. The order isn't as old as 1287."

Larry tapped his head and thought some more. It was amazing how many interesting things you could learn when you dug even just a little below the surface of a problem. For Larry it was usually history or languages, but it must be the same feeling Neil and Angel got looking at the work of great chefs. "Well, maybe that Cordon Bleu order came out of another order? An older one? But nobody wrote that history down? This could be the old old old symbol that they refined as they got more, I don't know, organized."

"Possibly," Angel said. "But why did the people who wrote in this book feel they had to hide the symbol? You said it didn't show up until the book got wet."

"Yeah, it wasn't written in ink. Some words were, but other words and dates and the symbol were all hidden." Larry reached for a rolled-up poster-sized paper on the side of the desk. He pushed the book aside and unfurled the paper on the desk. He had written the names, numbers, and symbols in rows.

"I've been looking for a pattern. Look here at the first row. Pierre wrote a weird farewell note. He ends with his name and the dates 1272–1311, but he left a big blank space in between."

"So those dates might indicate when this Pierre lived and died."

"That seems pretty standard, although he wrote 1311 himself, which seems kinda weird to know the date of your own death."

Angel considered for a moment. "Maybe he was dying when he wrote the note? There is that short letter before the recipes where he says farewell to Irina somebody."

"Sure. But the real question is, why the blank space?"

"And?"

"The answer is that the space wasn't really blank. When the pages got wet, it revealed other words, numbers, and symbols in between the dates. So look at the page." Larry took his finger and followed the line of ink and raised paper symbols.

"So now there's a pattern. It starts with Pierre 1272 in ink. But when the page is wet we can see that the letter F and the date 1287 actually come next. That's followed by the name Valette on top of a circle-and-cross symbol. Then the symbol shows up with an x through it and the date 12-something—the paper's a little torn there, or maybe burned. Then the name Valette shows up again with the date 1293. Then we finish with the date 1311.

"The symbol refers to a person, maybe—this Valette, perhaps—or maybe some kind of event?"

"But it's not just Pierre F. The pattern is pretty much followed for all the other entries. Nicholas F. Genevieve F. The dates move a little, but not much." Larry pointed to another row, about halfway down the paper.

"Look, here's Patrice F, 1720–1747, written in ink."

"The 1747 is in someone else's handwriting, so even more likely a death date."

Larry nodded. "And then Neil got the page wet, revealing stuff in between the dates. There's the *F* and then date 1735. Then there's the date 1737, the symbol with Valette overtop, and then it ends with 1747 in ink."

"Hmmm. The first entry, Pierre's, is the only one with the symbol crossed out," Angel said, scratching his beard.

"Yeah. Pierre F. Weird, huh? Kind of weird stuff to hide in a recipe book, don't ya think?"

"It's a family tree." It was Neil's voice. Larry swung around and Angel looked up. Neil was leaning on the door frame, groggy but awake. Isabella walked up behind him and adjusted the blanket over his shoulders.

"You look like carp," Larry joked.

"Ha, ha," Neil said. "You see yourself in the mirror every day, so I guess you're an expert."

"Can you two act like grown-ups for *una minute, per favore?*" Isabella said.

"Fine," Larry said. "Okay, cousin. You say it's a family tree?"

"Yes, our family tree. The *F* stands for Flambé."

Larry looked at the pattern. "Um, maybe. It could also be frankfurter. Why do you think it's Flambé?"

"It has to be. These are all great chefs, amazing chefs, all with *F*s next to their names. For some reason they didn't want to spell out their full names, but the chefs in this book are geniuses."

"Just like you, I suppose?" Larry rolled his eyes.

Neil nodded. "Thanks for noticing."

"I was kidding!"

"There's more. Angel said he was told to give me the book on my fifteenth birthday."

"So?" Larry didn't follow.

"Look at the numbers. 1272–1287. The difference? Fifteen years. The first date is the year the chef was born. The second is when they turned fifteen."

"That is when the symbol shows up in Pierre's line," Larry said, looking at the pattern.

Neil nodded. "These chefs were fifteen when something happened. The other dates refer to other big events."

"So why not just write the symbol down? Why hide it?"

"Angel said the phone message mentioned a curse. The symbol could represent that curse, when it began. I think maybe it had to do with their cooking, their ability to cook. They lost it, or someone made sure they couldn't cook, or they lost their restaurants or whatever they had in 1723. That's the curse . . . maybe."

"What could our teenage ancestors have done that would have ticked off somebody that much?"

"No idea."

"I mean, don't get me wrong, you are an expert at making enemies. Maybe it runs in the family . . . that and good looks, of course. I got those." Larry winked at Isabella who smacked him on the head.

"Do you really believe in curses?" Isabella asked.

"I don't know," Neil said. "But I've been trying to work out why such great chefs had to make do with such meager ingredients. Maybe the answer is that they were prevented from cooking anything else."

"Because they were cursed?"

"Maybe that's how the curse, whatever it is, works?" Neil's mind was grasping to make sense of the idea. He got more agitated as he tried to piece it all together. "Look, I just turned fifteen. Now Picón wants me to duel DBC. If I lose, I agree never to cook again. Maybe the symbol pops up when there's been a battle or duel, or something—"

"—that a Flambé loses," Larry finished the sentence. "What an illustrious family legacy."

"I'm not going to lose!" Neil yelled.

Isabella touched Neil's shoulder to calm him. "So you think DBC is trying to carry on this curse."

"Possibly."

"And if you win, you'll break a thousand years of your family history? If it's a curse, you'll break the curse?"

Neil rubbed his forehead in frustration. "I don't know. I don't know."

Larry looked at the time lines on the paper thoughtfully. "Neil could be right. The chefs turn fifteen and then get noticed, like Neil did on TV for the Azteca Cocina—and then they get taken down."

"So for Pierre," Isabella said slowly, looking at the pages in front of her, "the symbol shows up right away—so maybe someone noticed him right after he turned fifteen," Isabella said.

Neil looked at the paper. "Maybe that's what the symbol means. It's when this Valette person, or whatever Valette is, noticed him."

". . . or decided to come after him?" Angel said.

Larry nodded. "Okay, maybe. So then Pierre got noticed right away, like you. Most of the others got noticed later, *after* they turned fifteen. So that's when something happens. Curse, lost duel, hangnail . . . whatever."

Neil shrugged. "Maybe the sequence is birth date, fifteenth birthday, then the curse, and then . . . death?"

Larry looked at his notes. "Then the date of the curse is when they stopped cooking, or had to stop cooking real food and turned to roadkill and rodents. And it has something to do with the name Valette and that symbol?"

Neil said nothing.

"I don't believe in curses," Isabella said, frowning.

Jones nodded. "Me neither, but I'm a strong believer in revenge, and DBC seems bent on that. Maybe this Picón character found out about the curse and is using it to mess with your brain."

"Or nose," Larry said.

Neil walked back into the dining room, feeling frustrated. He couldn't cook. His restaurant was still closed. In a few days he was going to face a huge decision—duel Deep Blue Cheese or skip it and call Picón's bluff—with his future on the line.

Something near the door caught his eye. It was an

envelope. He walked over and stared down at the clean white surface. He hadn't noticed it there before. He looked around. The door didn't have a mail slot and there were no gaps.

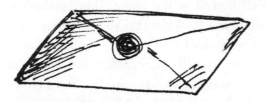

Neil tried the handle. The door was still locked from the inside. How could someone have left a note inside his dining room without him noticing? Neil picked up the note and sniffed it. It was cotton-fiber, but otherwise there was no other smell.

He opened it. It appeared to be a blank piece of paper. He held it up to the light. The faintest suggestion of a shadow rippled across the page. Neil looked around and grabbed a glass of water from one of the tables. He poured it on the envelope and the paper.

His eyes grew wide as the circle-and-cross symbol emerged from the soaking envelope.

The wet paper revealed a note.

> Be on guard. Protect the book. The curse is real. Do not go to Paris.

"Paris? Who the heck ever suggested I go to Paris?" Neil stood, utterly confused, watching as the paper began to dry and the mysterious message disappeared.

He stared once more out of his front window. The road crew had parked the bulldozer right in front of the storefront across the street. But through the cab he could see the front door of Carrion. The two blue lights were staring back at him, he was sure of it. "Blue lights," he said. He slammed his fist on the nearest table. "I know you're in there, Picón. I'm coming to get you." He ran back in the kitchen and grabbed a knife.

Chapter Eleven

Swiss Cheesed

Sean Nakamura stood on the sidewalk outside Chez Flambé and looked back across the street. The shabby Pets and Pelts sign was in serious danger of falling off the equally shabby building. Underneath, the interior was pitch-black, revealing nothing. The proposed new Carrion restaurant was a mystery to Sean, and he didn't like that. He'd gone through the usual channels and hadn't been able to turn up any information on who owned the place.

So Sean had turned to the *unusual* channels—doing some research on his own time with contacts that weren't always good company for a cop on company time. One thing he'd been able to turn up was the original owner, Jack Russell. Jack had sold the place about a month before, it turned out. He hadn't been looking to sell, but then a strange man showed up at his apartment with a blank check from a Swiss bank. Jack took the money and ran, literally, to the best dives the Pacific Northwest had to offer. But Nakamura had been able to track him down.

Nakamura rang the Chez Flambé doorbell. There was no sound. "Broken? After all that cash Neil sunk into the place?" he wondered. He knocked on the door and waited.

Nakamura had also done some asking around to see if anyone was trying to pawn a safe with recipes in it, but no leads there. He hoped Neil would appreciate the effort, but he wasn't expecting much gratitude.

He was right. "Oh, look, it's Inspector I'm-Too-Busy-to-Help," Neil said, opening the door. He was holding a knife and looked angry.

"I guess that makes you Chef I'm-Too-Annoying-to-Let-You-In?"

"It makes me curious if you've actually done any police work since you shut my restaurant down."

"Actually, I have been doing some digging around."

"Find anything useful . . . for a change?"

"I'll take that as a 'thanks,'" Sean said, a little peeved, but not surprised. He pulled out his notebook and flipped it open. "I don't have a lot. I know that someone with a Swiss bank account bought the property a year ago."

"The owner is Swiss? Sounds like a story with a lot of holes," Larry said, joining them in the doorway.

Nakamura groaned. "No. Swiss banks are notorious for their secrecy—so the actual owner could be from anywhere. The old owner did meet the guy with the check and thought he came from France, or maybe Germany, possibly Italy . . . or Albania. . . ."

"Thanks for narrowing it down to Europe." Larry laughed. "We only have to search one continent."

"Yeah, not much of a lead," Nakamura admitted.

"We can assume the new owner wants to remain anonymous, and was willing to pay above the market value for the place."

Neil narrowed his eyes. "Or maybe the guy had a Spanish accent? Like the kind a crazy Latin-American computer programmer might have?" Neil suggested.

"Um, what?" Nakamura asked, totally confused.

Larry stepped forward. "A guy named Stanley Picón is after Neil. He's a computer programmer. Hates Neil."

Nakamura nodded slowly. "And you think he's living over in that place?"

Neil kept his eyes riveted on the blue lights. "Let's just say that I've got an inkling there's more in that dump than empty space and old hats."

They stared over at the darkened window.

"Like a computer programmer," Nakamura said, "from Latin America? He needs to find a better apartment."

"Maybe. We can't prove it from out here. So maybe we should go break in," Neil said. "If there's no one there, we leave. If Picón is there we can force him to admit he poisoned the critics. Maybe my safe is in there somewhere as well."

"I'm in," said Larry with a smile and a shrug.

"I'm not," Nakamura said. "You're honestly suggesting, to an officer of the law, that we break and enter a private property?"

"I thought you said you're too busy to even investigate B-and-E's in this part of town?"

"Don't get cute."

"Yeah, that's my job." Larry smiled.

"Never mind," Neil said. "I'll do it myself."

"Neil . . . ," Nakamura began warningly.

Before Nakamura could finish, Neil had marched across the street to the restaurant, clutching the knife. He stopped at the door and looked around. The street was deserted. He wondered for the thousandth time why he owned a restaurant in this part of town. He leaned down to slide the knife into the lock. As he turned the handle, the door opened with a creak. "You're kidding!" he said. "I've been staring at this stupid place for a week and the stupid door wasn't even locked?!" He kicked it all the way open.

"Nose, don't go in there!" Nakamura yelled. He turned to Larry. "What's wrong with your idiot cousin?"

For once, Larry didn't reply with a wisecrack. "He's not himself lately. He's been a weirder, slightly unstable version of himself. To be honest, I'm worried about him."

"Well, let's go get him before he does something stupid."

They ran across the street as Neil walked through the door.

Two small blue dots stared back at him from the back wall.

"Deep Blue Cheese!" Neil shouted. "I'm here and I'm going to dismantle you chip by chip." He held the knife in front of him and rushed toward the lights.

Immediately high-pitched sirens began to scream. "Ahhhhhhh!" Neil clutched his ears. Lights flashed on and off. Stuffed animal heads stared back blankly from the wall, many wearing odd hats. Empty cages stood stacked against the wall and on the counters. Neil wasn't sure, but there seemed to be small animal skeletons in more than a few. This wasn't a restaurant; it was a house of horrors!

The sirens continued to wail. Neil spied the two dots on the back wall. They weren't human or computer. They were merely the lights of a motion sensor alarm, reflecting off the glassy eyes of a stuffed ferret.

The lights kept flashing and Neil noticed something else that made his heart leap. The floor was moving.

Hundreds, maybe thousands, of rats, frightened by the sound and light show, were scurrying from the doors and out of every crack and crevice in the walls. Neil's eyes grew wide as he faced the onslaught of the hideous, living shag carpet. He dropped his knife. It fell to the floor and disappeared into the furry mass.

"Nose, get out of there!" Nakamura yelled from the doorway.

Neil could feel the swarm of rodents running over his sneakers. He looked up and saw even more of them pouring out of the doorway that led to the basement stairs. He bolted as fast as he could for the door, but stepped on something that gave an audible and pained "squeak." Neil lost his footing and spun around.

"Don't fall down, whatever you do," Larry yelled. The lights stopped flashing, the sirens kept wailing.

Which way was Neil facing now? Where was the door? He took a step forward and walked face-first into a giant spiderweb.

"Ahhhhhh!" he yelled, desperately scratching at his face.

"Nose, this way!" It was Nakamura, barely audible over the din. Neil did his best to follow the sound of Nakamura's voice. Rats continued to squeak as he quickly brought his foot down in his rush to escape. He could feel the angry rodents nibbling at the rubber soles of his sneakers.

"Neil!" Larry yelled. "Pretend they're toys! Just harmless little squeaky toys!"

Neil closed his eyes and made a final rush for the door, leaping out ahead of the final wave of rats. A flood of rats swept by, and then continued down the street. The door slammed shut.

Larry and Nakamura clung to the side of the building, watching the twitching tails pour down the street before disappearing around the corner.

Neil lay absolutely still on the sidewalk, his eyes closed and his heaving chest the only sign he was alive.

Larry walked over and nudged him with his toe. "Neil, you okay?"

Neil gave out a miserable moan.

"Good. So . . . no supercomputer inside there, I take it?"

Neil moaned again.

"So, it's just a dumpy building?"

Neil propped himself up

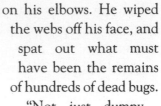

on his elbows. He wiped the webs off his face, and spat out what must have been the remains of hundreds of dead bugs.

"Not just dumpy— disgusting. . . . It reminded me of your apartment." Neil stood up and began shaking the dust and dirt (and he didn't want to know what else) off his clothes.

Nakamura walked right up to him, waving his arms in the air. "You idiot! Never EVER run into a situation without the lights on! You want to get yourself killed?"

"Right now, that might be an improvement," Neil said, picking some more indeterminate crud out of his hair.

Nakamura put his hand on Neil's shoulder. "You know, Neil, this place may have absolutely nothing to do with this computer guy or anything. Maybe it's just a dump that some nutty chef wants to turn into a restaurant."

"I guess the rats found something to eat in there," Larry said, staring back at the closed door. "Maybe Carrion is a restaurant for rodents?"

"It's not a restaurant for anyone. No one has done anything to that place. It should be condemned! "

Larry chuckled. "Yeah, you said the same thing about Chez Flambé. But now look at it!"

"I'd rather not," Neil said. He looked at his empty hand. "Oh, no! I dropped my knife back in there."

"You grabbed one of your good knives to jimmy a door lock? You really are rattled there, cuz," Larry said.

Then Neil looked down at his feet. One of his sneakers had fallen off in his attempt to escape the rats.

"I've got to go back. I think the rats are all gone." Neil walked to the door, grabbed the handle and promptly smashed face-first into the now locked door. "Ouch!" he cried as he stepped back, grabbing his throbbing nose.

"Ouch! Great! Just what I needed," he said. He peered through the grimy glass door window. He could just make out the two blue dots of light fading. "I'm willing to bet DBC International doesn't just install cooling equipment. I'll bet they also do motion sensors and remote door locks." He turned to face Nakamura, a trickle of blood sliding out of his nostril.

"Look, Nose, I'll keep digging and see what I can find out."

"Good. I've got a duel to prep for." Then he kicked the door one more time and stormed back across the street.

He stopped in front of his door and lowered his head.

"Rats," he said.

"Yeah, we know," Larry said, catching up. "You still smell like them."

"No, I mean, 'Rats, I've just realized something else that's all wrong.'"

"What could be worse than the day you've had?"

Neil turned his head and looked straight into Larry's eyes, his nose still trickling blood. "I have gym class tomorrow, and these are my only pair of sneakers."

Peter 1900

Peter Flambé was cursed. He had to be—there was no other explanation for the number of horrible things that had happened to him as he'd struggled to be a great chef.

Peter stared at his restaurant—smoke and flames pouring from the skeletal remains of the kitchen as the Cheektowaga fire department busily pumped water onto the inferno. This was the third inexplicable fire at his restaurant this year. And this was his third restaurant in a

decade, each failing more spectacularly than the last.

But this time it had been way too close a call. He and his family lived upstairs. He had barely gotten them out, barely gotten the neighbors out and all of them across the street before the gas lines that fed the lamps and the stoves sent a giant ball of blue flame hurtling toward the clouds.

The resulting crater was now foiling the best efforts of the horse-drawn pumping crews. The bigger cities now had faster, horseless fire engines that could respond more quickly to disasters such as this one, but Peter was sure it wouldn't have made a difference. His life here was over, as finished as the building that he'd called his home.

Another blast sent the horses rearing back in fear, their masters struggling to calm them and keep the hoses aimed at the inferno.

Why did he keep trying? He'd been happy and successful when he'd been young. At fifteen he'd been the youngest head chef ever hired at the Brasserie Buffalo, the best restaurant west of Europe. He'd excelled, grown up, grown wealthy, fallen in love.

Then after the Great War, everything changed. Patrons at BB complained of food sickness, odd tastes, bad ingredients, and worse. He was fired. He tried again and again to start his own restaurants. Everything would work for a while, but then the same complaints would return.

Peter tore off his apron and threw it into the growing puddle of blackened mud. This was it. This was the end. Cooking had been his passion, his life—but no more.

Peter looked over at his infant son, John, cradled in the arms of his wife, Ivy. Peter swore an oath at that moment. John would never see the inside of a kitchen. Peter would make sure that he and his children and his children's children would never even suspect there was any allure to a properly seasoned chicken thigh, or the tantalizing aroma of fresh-baked bread. If possible, he would make John hate gourmet food.

Times were changing anyway. Food was now just fuel for the glorious citizens of the glorious future. Cars were speeding up the pace of life. Food was going to come in packages—instant oatmeal, chocolate, tea in a bag. Peter had even helped create new food bars for the troops who had fought so bravely and futilely in Europe. Hundreds had nibbled on Flambé bars in the bunkers of France. No, the future didn't need chefs.

John was going to eat modern food. He was going to be an accountant, a lawyer, a mechanic—anything but a chef. Peter wouldn't even tell him about the world of haute cuisine. Peter would strive to make sure he was absolutely ignorant of how to cook.

The acrid black smoke turned to white steam, a sign the firefighters were gaining the upper hand . . . but for Peter there was nothing left to save or regret. . . . He placed his hand on Ivy's shoulder and led her away, toward the train station.

They'd move again. Peter had seen pictures of the glorious mountains out west. There was gold out there, somewhere, and a chance to make a new life.

As he turned his family away from the carnage, he remembered his notebook. In his hurry to escape the flames he'd left it inside his safe. He didn't look back. What did it matter? The notebook, like his old life, was nothing more than ashes now.

"Where are we heading?" Ivy asked as they arrived on the platform, watching as a huge steam engine pulled into the station. John stayed cradled in her arms, sucking his thumb.

Peter turned to the ticket clerk behind the metal-barred window. "What's the last stop on this train?"

The man checked the map. "Last stop is a place called Vancouver."

"We'll take three tickets."

"Round-trip?"

Peter looked at his son, and at the glimmering silver train that would take them all away from their old life. "No. One-way."

Chapter Twelve

Gym Nauseam

Neil opened the door the smallest of cracks and peered into the gym. Billy Berger stood at center court, clutching a red rubber ball with his meaty fingers so hard that it created ripples in the surface. Billy didn't blink as he stared at the doorway, smirking . . . waiting, Neil was certain, for the first strand of red hair to emerge from the boys' locker room.

Neil let out a deep sigh. He had been able to avoid gym class for the entire term so far, thanks to hand-delivered boxfuls of his patented Neil Flambé energy bars—personally designed to help Coach Pitts through his fall marathon training. But then Pitts had twisted an ankle slipping on a banana peel someone had left on the track, and no longer had any use for energy bars. No amount of whining was going to get Neil out of class today.

Neil Flambé was not out of shape, not at all. Running a restaurant is a draining business. Neil got plenty of exercise sprinting between food stations, lifting joints of meat, chopping vegetables, and grabbing hot pots of boiling water and pans of spitting oil. He also ate well.

But Neil was not athletically coordinated. He also had zero interest in using wood to smack a piece of rubber ("wood is meant for my pizza oven") or football ("the only pigskin I care about is *chicharron* and a good salsa verde"). This attitude didn't exactly make him popular with the jock set at school—not that anything else about Neil did either. He'd once made a vain effort to improve the drinks in the water bottles with his home-carbonator and some fresh pomegranate juice. Coach Pitts's favorite white tracksuit still showed the purple stains from the resulting sideline spewfest.

It had cost Neil an extra three cartons of energy bars to smooth over that one.

He'd also gone through a growth spurt recently and his shorts and shirt looked ridiculously small on his gangly frame. He had a sense of foreboding that whatever happened as soon as he stepped through that door was going to be yet more evidence that his fifteenth birthday had triggered a one-thousand-year-old curse.

The door swung open suddenly, yanking Neil out of the locker room and onto the gym floor. He lifted his arms to defend himself. Instead of punches, he was immediately assaulted with the shrill call of a whistle.

"You got a problem, Flambé?" It was

Coach Pitts, standing over him with his arms akimbo and the whistle between his lips poised to fire again.

Neil stared past the coach to Berger who was standing behind him, grinning and passing the ball back and forth between his hands.

"No problem," Neil said, raising himself up slowly. On a normal day Neil would have retorted with a snarky comeback like "None you can help me with, unless you can tell the difference between a tomatillo and ground cherry." (Larry was always telling him he needed "a little more zing" in his comebacks.) But his usual swagger was gone. He was, as Larry put it, "knocked for a loop" by everything that had happened to him since his birthday fiasco.

"No problem . . . COACH," Coach said.

"No problem, Coach," Neil repeated.

Coach Pitts turned around and ran to the far end of the court, blowing his whistle with each step. His departure erased the only obstacle between Berger and Neil.

"The game is basketball!" Coach yelled from the opposite end of the gym. "Not rugby. We'll start by practicing. Everyone pick a partner."

Neil watched as every other kid in the class stared at Berger nervously and then sidled away to team up elsewhere. Neil knew right away Berger had rigged it—with money or violence—to ensure he got Neil.

Berger clutched the ball, his lips curling up in a menacing smile.

Coach Pitts blew his whistle. "All, right, remember to pass the ball softly. You want the other guy to

catch it on a run." Neil saw that as his cue to start running.

"Run back and forth. Call for the pass. Flambé, you've got to call for the pass. Pretend you're rushing for the basket."

The only basket Neil Flambé ever rushed for in his life contained a dozen summer sausages a stray dog had grabbed from him at the Trout Lake market. But he figured the more he moved, the less chance there was that Berger would hit him with a direct shot.

Coach yelled again. "Berger, hit him with the pass, c'mon!" Neil wished Coach hadn't used the phrase "hit him."

Berger grinned. "I have waited so long for this, fenu-geek."

Fenu-geek? Neil was so amazed that he actually stopped running. Had Billy Berger just made a food joke? Something smelled fishy, and it wasn't just the socks he'd borrowed from Larry. *How's that for zing?* Neil thought as he watched Berger draw his arm back and release the ball like a howitzer, right at Neil's head.

"Oh, no," Neil said, his feet frozen to the spot. Everything seemed to happen in slow motion. Berger released the ball. It flew through the air.

The ball struck him with such force that he fell back onto the floor and slid a good five feet. His nose, still throbbing from his accidental turn as a door-knocker the night before, took the full brunt of the throw and made a sickening crunch.

He sat up against the wall mat and grabbed his face. More blood, a too-common occurrence these days, colored his fingers. His head swam with a mixture of pain and a new feeling for him: resignation.

This was the curse at work. He was being made to suffer. Fate was working through idiots like Picón and Berger to tear him down. That's what it was. The cosmos was jealous. He was paying for his tremendous skills. This was all making sense. Thanks to his sense of smell and his superior intellect, Neil had sent Berger to jail, and now Berger was getting his revenge. His superiority in the kitchen had made other chefs jealous, and now they were out to get him. Everyone was out to get him. And whether it was thanks to some supernatural spell or good old human jealousy, they were winning.

Well, why not just give in? Neil had done more than anyone thought possible for a fifteen-year-old. Maybe he had run his course. His ambition aimed at much higher goals, but with the world against him, and apparently the universe, what could he do?

Through the blur and the pain in his nose, Neil could hear the sound of Coach Pitts's whistle and Berger's laughter. Then a new thought struck him: Tomorrow he had to fight DBC. But now he couldn't smell a thing. He was dead meat.

Larry nudged Neil in the ribs. "C'mon, chef-boy. Get it in gear. You have a duel tomorrow!" Neil looked completely dejected and utterly defeated. Larry tried more cajoling. "Neil Flambé give in? Ludicrous! I've seen you fight crazy Aztecs and murderous chefs, and win underground duels in Venice, New York, Regina. . . ."

Neil laid his forehead down on the counter and began banging it slowly. "There's no way I can win this stupid thing. I can't smell. Apparently I can't cook. I . . . I don't know what to say . . . what to do. . . ."

Luckily, his nose hadn't been completely busted. A quick, and painful, pinch from the school nurse had set the bone back in place and Neil could faintly pick up aromas. But the swelling was still there. He kept holding ice packs against his nose, and it seemed to be helping, but would it be enough?

He could just blow off the duel, of course. Isabella was safe. The canisters were disintegrated so there was no way to pin anything on DBC. But if he did that he'd have to (a) admit defeat, something Neil hated to do, and (b) give up Chez Flambé. As much as he hated the restaurant, he knew he needed it as a stepping stone to the next level. He was bleeding money, and being closed he wasn't bringing any new money in to the business. The money Picón was offering was exactly what he needed to survive. There was also an implied (c) that Picón would exact another kind of revenge if Neil didn't show. He *had* to duel.

But Neil's practice round was an unmitigated disaster. He'd invited Jones, Isabella, and Angel to sit in the dining room for a taste test. He didn't tell them it was for the duel, but said he wanted to try out some new dishes for when the restaurant finally reopened.

Picón had laid out the rules—Neil could bring the ingredients for one of the two dishes for the duel. So, to prepare, he'd made his five best meals. His five "can't miss" dishes—pommes de terre à la Flambé, salmon with dill and wild rice, risotto, prawns and garlic, pizza con funghi . . . It was no use.

Every meal seemed great once he'd plated it, even with his compromised sense of smell. But once the meals were delivered to his waiting jury members—Angel, Isabella, and Jones—something went wrong. They'd each tasted the dishes then shoved their plates aside with looks of disgust and disappointment.

"The AC is off," Neil said to Larry. "What could be wrong?" He'd even thrown a plate full of expensive salmon pâté through the back window rather than bring it out to more bad reviews.

Angel tried to keep him focused. "Try again. Every chef hits bumps in the road. It happens."

"Not to me," Neil said angrily.

Isabella got up and walked over to Neil.

"I don't need a hug," Neil said.

"Good," she said. "Because I'm not here to give you one." She grabbed his chef's hat and hit him over the head with it.

"Ouch!" Neil said.

Isabella stared hard into Neil's eyes. "Are you a chef or a pathetic little bambino? If you want to be my friend, let alone my boyfriend, you had better show a little more backbone. Now get in there and cook. I'll be waiting for my next dish." Then she stormed back to the judging table and crossed her arms.

Larry stood by the door, rolling with laughter. "I didn't know Isabella was secretly a football coach."

Neil rubbed his head and walked past Larry into the kitchen. "More like a linebacker. At least she didn't whack me in the nose," he said.

"Well, truth is, cousin, you probably need a little butt-kicking. I've never seen you so low."

Neil took a deep breath. He still didn't know what was wrong, but if the people around him were going to put in an effort, he had to at least try one more dish.

"Okay," he said, standing up. "One last try. We're going to make a simple and fast appetizer. Bruschetta."

"Finger food?"

"With a twist. We'll use some of Angel's goat cheese mozzarella with my prosciutto and the secret ingredient." Neil pulled out the remains of his truffle oil.

"Didn't you try that stuff on Chili?" Larry asked.

Neil hesitated. He had tried it on the critic and it had not gone well. Where was Chili? Neil could have used his

expertise right now, his expert sense of what made a great meal. But he had disappeared. "Chili is gone and this oil is excellent. I know it is." He began to slice a loaf of crusty bread. "Toast these with a hint of butter, then rub them with garlic. I'll chop some basil and tomato."

Larry nodded.

The dish was prepped in just minutes. Isabella was still glaring at the kitchen door as Neil made his way in with the tray of appetizers.

He carefully placed a dish in front of each judge.

"They smell delicious," Angel said, taking a long whiff.

"Especially the cheese," Larry said with a wink.

"You have very good taste . . . in cheese." Angel nodded, staring disapprovingly at Larry's constantly disheveled chef's jacket. He picked up a slice, carefully balancing it in his hand so that none of the toppings slid off.

"Shall we all try it together?" he said to Isabella and Jones.

"I don't think I can be so . . . coordinated," Isabella said, carefully cutting a slice with her knife and balancing the morsel on her fork.

"You certainly don't need any stains on that nice shawl," Jones said, delicately cutting his own slice. Neil gazed at his enormous hands and wondered how that was even possible.

"On three, then," Angel said. "One, two, three."

He popped the lot into his mouth and immediately smiled. "Sublime," he said, closing his eyes and savoring the wonderful combination of textures and tastes.

"Blech," Isabella and Jones said together, spitting their samples back out onto their plate.

Neil was utterly confused. He stared from face to face. "Which is it? Great or horrible?"

"Great," said Angel.

"Horrible," said Jones and Isabella.

Neil looked down at the plates. The dishes were identical. There was no way they could taste that different.

"Maybe Angel got the lucky one?" Larry wondered. Angel reached over and grabbed Isabella's bruschetta. He took a bite out of the crusty bread. "This is fantastic," he said. He did the same to Jones's with the same response.

"Let me try yours," Isabella said. Angel passed her the plate and she sliced a mouthful and lifted it to her mouth. As soon as it touched her tongue she gagged. "It tastes like salt," she said, putting the forkful back on the plate.

Something clicked in Neil's brain. Larry had been right when he'd said there were other problems besides DBC's air conditioning sabotage. It also hit him like a ton of briquettes where he had seen the symbol before. He grabbed the fork from Isabella and turned it over.

There, stamped right into the silver, where the stem met the tines, was a tiny cross inside a circle.

"ARGH!" Neil stabbed the fork right into the tabletop, digging the tines a full inch into the wood.

"Neil, what is wrong?" Isabella said, sliding her chair away from the table and Neil. Jones began to stand up, clenching his fists.

Neil didn't answer. He ran from table to table, flipping the cutlery like a madman. Each piece was the same, bearing the mark.

He lifted one of the tables and sent all the forks, knives, glasses, and plates crashing to the floor. Spent, he sat down on the floor. He looked at the faces of his friends, all of them now standing up and staring at him.

"Neil. What is going on?" Isabella asked. Neil needed to be careful in answering that question. He'd taken Picón at his word when he'd said there'd been only one hidden camera. He'd searched for more and found nothing, but he needed to be absolutely sure.

"Hey, chef-boy. Isabella asked you a question," Jones said, pounding his fist into his palm.

"Yeah, cousin. You've been acting weird lately. But this takes the cake."

Neil sniggered. Cake. Yes, that should have been the tip-off. Neil was now certain that the forks were killing his dishes, tainting them somehow. He also knew right away that the duel with DBC was supposed to happen right here, at Chez Flambé, using these rigged utensils. DBC was fighting dirty. Fine. He'd fight dirty too . . . and he'd win.

"Larry, I give up," he said as loud as possible. "I don't know what's wrong. I'll never win tomorrow." Then he ran back into the kitchen and out the back door.

Sure enough, just a minute later Larry followed him outside and found Neil pacing up and down behind the trash bin. The cats followed him like his own private feline posse.

"Where are the others?" Neil said as Larry walked up to him.

Larry was expecting to find Neil banging his head again, so he wasn't quite sure what to make of the gleam

in Neil's eye. "I apologized for you, again, and they went home."

"Good." Neil nodded. And he actually gave a small smile. "Good."

"I have to say that Isabella's not too impressed with the return of the bambino chef."

"I'm not being a crybaby."

"Um, I don't think she'll appreciate you hoodwinking her by acting like one either."

Neil felt a pang of guilt. "Yeah, well. I'll have to deal with that later. I just needed to make sure that no one suspected."

"Suspected what?"

Neil looked suspiciously at the cats. "How do we know those are real?"

"What? The cats? Are you losing it?"

"What if those are robot cats . . . sent to spy on us?"

Larry looked at the cats, many of them licking their paws and other places. "I've watched those tubs of lard grow from kittens to furry bowling balls. They're real. You're the one acting like a robot."

Neil shook his head. Of course he was being paranoid. Still . . . "Larry, grab your bike. I'll tell you my plan on the way."

"What? Way? Where?"

Neil smiled again. "We're going hunting."

Chapter Thirteen

Just Fondue It

Neil sat in his kitchen, tapping his fingers impatiently on his seat—a giant red cooler. It was the type of cooler he sometimes took on picnics, picnics where patrons paid plenty for Neil's selection of maple-smoked salmon and grilled "lamburger with limburger" (or flamburgers as Larry called them). Today the cooler contained his secret ingredient for the biggest battle of his life.

The clock ticked closer to eight.

Neil softly touched the end of his nose. His sense of smell was bouncing back, but it was far from perfect. Neil wasn't sure what upgrades Picón had added to his stupid bucket of silicon and transistors, but he was certain that tonight would not be as simple as his last battle with Deep Blue Cheese.

The clock struck eight and shook Neil out of his thoughts. Neil heard the back door creak open. He didn't turn around.

"Hello, Stanley. Ready to lose?"

"Cocky as ever," Picón said with a scoff.

"Can you help me with my cooler? I assume there's a van on the way to take us to our duel."

"Oh, no," Stanley said. "I think we will stay here for our little duel. Your last meal should be at home."

Neil shook his shoulders. He hoped it gave Picón the impression he was surprised. Thank goodness he had his back to Picón. Neil suppressed his smirk and turned around. Stanley Picón was standing in the doorway wearing a large overcoat.

"Where's your computer?" Neil asked

"This time our duel will be a little different." Stanley swung off the coat and revealed his body, which was a mass of mechanical joints and wires, all connected to a glowing black and blue pack on his chest. It was hard to tell where the wires ended and the human began.

"Who are you supposed to be, Cast-Iron Man?" Neil didn't need to fake surprise at this turn of events.

"DBC and I are one." Picón grimaced menacingly. Neil saw with a jolt that some of the wires went directly into Stanley's head.

"You're insane," Neil said.

Picón laughed and Neil could see sparks shooting from his hair, sort of like one of those electro-balls he'd seen at the science museum.

"This is the future, you little jerk. DBC will be sending me all the information, all the signals, and I will perform the cooking. I will use my own nose and taste to make the adjustments. You don't stand a chance."

"That's what you said last time." Neil could feel his anger rising. "How'd that work out for you?"

"Your tricks won't work this time," Picón said,

pulling a large knife from somewhere in the back of the blinking unit and quickly honing it on a metal rod.

Neil grabbed his favorite knife from his magnetic rack and did the same. "Okay robocook, let's get started. And I hope you brought the money. I have a loan payment due tomorrow."

"I know you do. And when you miss it, you'll lose the restaurant."

"Did your stupid computer hack into the bank database to figure that one out?" Neil scoffed.

Stanley twitched. Neil thought he heard a sharp electronic zap.

"No more chitchat," Stanley said, striding into the middle of the kitchen. "It is time to cook."

Neil looked around.

"Where are the judges?"

Stanley pointed to the kitchen doors. Neil walked over and peered through the window. His eyes grew wide. Seated in his restaurant were three of the best chefs in the world—Gloria Chipotle, Gordon Hamsee, and Jamie Olive. They all looked surprised to see one another there and were exchanging smiles and slaps on the back . . . and what looked like postcards.

"How do I know you haven't paid them off?" Neil said.

"Do you really think those three need more money?"

Neil admitted it was unlikely. They were incredibly wealthy. Hamsee alone had dozens of Michelin starred restaurants spread all over the globe and sold a line of his own cookware.

"What are the cards they're passing around?"

"I sent each one of them this invitation yesterday, along with plane tickets and hotel accommodations," Picón said, handing Neil an embossed card that read:

The best meal of your life
is available tomorrow.

A duel for eternity,
and you are the judge.

All you have to do is
catch this flight.

"What chef could resist such an offer? There was no need to bribe them. You can trust that they will be impartial but incredibly tough. Perhaps you're afraid?"

Neil turned back to the kitchen. "Let's get started."

Stanley fired up the burners on his stove. "We will cook our first dish. DBC has chosen a personal favorite of his—*chou-fleur gratin, thon et thym avec une reduction vinaigrette.*"

Neil started. This was a recipe that usually took three days to properly prepare. Sauces had to be made. Tuna and cauliflower had to be marinated and chopped precisely. The recipe used almost every machine in the kitchen.

"You're nuts! When are the judges expecting to eat? Next week?"

"Oh, please. I happen to know that you have a container of marinated cauliflower in your walk-in fridge even as we speak."

Neil had to admit this was true. "So my fridge is a DBC original as well?"

Picón smiled. "Let's just say we know how to cool things down, and when to heat them up."

"Where's the camera in there?"

"Look inside the tuna can at the very back of the bottom tray. I swear it's the last one." Neil thought he heard a zap sound and Picón raised his hand as if he were swearing an oath. "It only tells me what's in the fridge, no microphone."

Something occurred to Neil. That fridge had contained a note a few weeks before warning him to stay away from Mexico. And he never used canned tuna. Was this a nod to Carlotta Calamari—the chef who'd become his mortal enemy after he'd exposed the canned tuna in her salade nicoise? How widespread was this curse conspiracy?

A loud buzzer sounded from Picón's chest, and the red numbers 30:00 appeared. "We have thirty minutes—starting now—to prepare the dish," Stanley said. He opened his cooler and grabbed his ingredients. He quickly chopped his cauliflower and threw the stalks into a pot of boiling water.

Neil ran into the fridge and pantry, scrambling to assemble the ingredients he needed for the dish. DBC, he knew, would follow the recipe as closely as possible. It was the way he—it—was programmed. Neil watched as Picón carefully measured out each small element for the dish, carefully waiting until his nose, and DBC circuitry, decided it was the perfect time to add them.

Neil, despite his anger, was impressed. Picón was right, DBC was going to be a more formidable foe.

Still, Neil knew he had to stick to his own way of cooking. He'd tricked DBC last time. This time it would have to come down to skill and creativity—and hoping that Picón didn't suspect Neil was on to his attempts to alter the taste of Neil's dishes with toxic cutlery.

Neil chopped his garlic. He smelled that DBC was using a mild garam masala with spices from South India. That was the traditional recipe that Neil knew. Neil could also tell that Picón wasn't using just any tuna, but a large piece of southern bluefin tuna, an endangered species.

What was Picón going to cook next, giant panda?

Neil *was* cheered by the fact he could smell the difference between that and his own albacore tuna. The pungent odors of the spices and the cooking were clearing a path up his nose, as gross as that image was. Neil looked down at the albacore and smiled again. It had a meatier texture than the poor rare specimen Picón was mechanically carving at the station next to him. His fish actually gave Neil a few more options for playing around with the recipe.

Neil rubbed his tuna steak with his own mixture of herbs and garlic, throwing in a small amount of nutmeg.

It was risky, because it could overpower a lesser fish, but Neil had balanced it perfectly—this time he was sure. Neil set the piece aside to concentrate on the vegetables.

Then he sniffed the air. Picón had added a smaller amount of the same spices to his fish! DBC wasn't just following a recipe—he was trying to match Neil's innovations. How was this possible?!

Neil looked over at Picón who smiled smugly. "This is the upgraded software and hardware."

Neil gritted his teeth and worked furiously. The clock wound down more quickly than Neil could have imagined. With five minutes left, he threw some oil in a hot pan and prepared to throw in his tuna. He was aware of Picón watching his every step. Neil stared at the tuna. His cauliflower au gratin was in the oven, almost ready to come out. The tuna needed something else, but he needed to keep Picón and DBC in the dark. He paused, and moved the pan off the heat.

"What are you doing?" Picón asked with a laugh. "Giving up?"

Neil grabbed a towel and raised it to his eyes. "I can't take it!" Neil said. He pretended to cry and turned and ran into his pantry, slamming the door behind him. He glanced back through the window and saw Picón grinning. Picón turned around and began to plate his tuna. Neil could even hear him humming happily. Or maybe that was the hum of DBC's hard drive.

Neil quickly ran to the back counter of the pantry and grabbed a small vial of rice wine vinegar. He'd bought it a year before at a private auction. It was one of a kind. Then another idea hit him. He grabbed some more vials and an empty bottle and, like a chemist, began to quickly mix and match his selection of liquids. He popped a cork into the bottle and then snuck it into his back pocket. He hoped his plan would work. Timing would be key.

Neil began to count down a full minute in his head. With each passing second he could feel the sweat forming on his forehead. This was going to be close, but he couldn't let Picón pick up on his plan until it was too late. Neil counted down to zero and then he stormed back into the kitchen and grabbed the skillet. He fired the flame on high and put the pan on the burner. Picón stared at him with a look of utter confusion.

Neil ran to the sink with his tuna and washed the herbed crust off as quickly as he could, then patted it dry. He grabbed a pair of tongs and headed straight back to the stove, the oil in the pan now spitting hot.

Picón yelled at Neil, "It's too late. You'll never finish in time!" and he laughed. But there was also a zap and Neil was certain he heard Picón's voice change and he hissed, apparently to himself, "You fool, he's changing his marinade!"

Neil didn't say a word. He threw the tuna into the pan. The oil was so hot that it spat small bits of liquid fire onto Neil's hands. He ignored the sharp pain and waited for the fish to smell just this side of cooked. Then he flipped it over and ran back to the oven. Neil quickly grabbed three of his cauliflower dishes and placed them on three plates.

Stanley looked at his own plates, already prepped

and ready for the judges. Then he looked down at his chest. There were only two minutes left.

"Should we change anything?" Picón said to his chest.

"No, it's too late, you idiot," he said in his other voice. "Let the boy shoot himself in the foot."

Neil ignored the argument and concentrated on his cooking. He laid his plates on the countertop next to the stove. The tuna continued to spit and snap in the pan. He quickly arranged a small salad of rocket and arugula on the dishes and then smelled. Picón's chest began to flash the final minute of cooking time.

Neil waited ten seconds, then he grabbed the bottle from his pocket, popped the cork off the top and threw the combined liquid into the pan with the tuna. Immediately the kitchen was filled with the aroma of rice wine vinegar, soy sauce, and mustard.

Picón mocked Neil. "That's not the recipe," he said, scowling.

"He's using vinegar. Add a dash more salt to our cauliflower," said the voice to Picón. Neil saw Picón's body jerk involuntarily toward the spice rack, grabbing a container of sea salt and crushing some over the tuna.

Twenty seconds.

Neil pulled one more vial from his pocket and threw a dash of heavy cream into the pot. It bubbled, sizzled, and steamed.

Ten seconds.

As quick as lightning Neil

used his tongs to pluck the tuna from the pan. It was down on his cutting board and sliced into three pieces with seven seconds left. He arranged the gloriously fragrant pieces of fish on top of the salad. With two seconds left, he spooned large dollops of the sauce on each piece of tuna.

Zero.

Neil stood up with a flourish and smiled at the three masterpieces that lay on the counter before him. Just enough of the spice rub had remained on the fish to add a slightly nutty flavor. But the cream and rice wine vinegar would perfectly complement the cheesy cauliflower that steamed away on the side.

Picón was shaking with anger. He could tell that Neil's dish was fabulous. Neil sighed. He could tell that Picón's dish was also excellent. At least Neil hadn't allowed DBC any time to adjust his dish to copy Neil's.

Which take on the dish would the judges prefer? Neil, for once, couldn't predict which way the competition would go. It was not a feeling he welcomed or understood.

Picón walked to the kitchen doors and flung them open. "There is to be no talking, just tasting and then judging," he said to the judges. The three chefs looked confused, but nodded.

"Now, we present!" Picón smiled. He grabbed his plates and strode back through the swinging doors.

"And may the best human being win," Neil said before following him into the dining room.

The three great chefs were inscrutable as they stared at the meals. They reached for their utensils. Neil smiled.

He had replaced the silverware with his old set of steel flatware. Whatever advantage Picón had hoped to enjoy was gone.

Neil couldn't resist pointing this out to Picón. "How do you like my OLD forks and knives?" He held one up to Picón's face.

Picón seemed completely uninterested. "Yes, they are fine," he said, not looking but just waving his hand. He was staring intently at the judges' faces.

Neil was taken aback. Surely Picón must have recognized that the silver had been changed? Neil felt a sense of panic. What if Picón had tampered with the old set as well? He licked his fork. It tasted fine. Maybe it only reacted to food?

But by all accounts the judges were impressed with both dishes. There were more than a few "wows" and moans of delight as they tasted the two different takes on the complicated recipe.

"No more tasting," Picón barked. He grabbed the plates back and then handed each judge a pencil and piece of paper. "Mark each dish out of ten for taste, presentation, and originali—"

He heard a few sharp zaps and saw Picón's face contorted with pain.

"I mean ten points for adherence to the original recipe!"

"What!?" Neil yelled. "That wasn't part of the competition!"

Picón's chest purred happily, a kind of computerized chuckle. "Must have slipped my mind. Come, let us wait in the kitchen for the verdict." Neil heard another zap and Picón's left arm grabbed Neil by the coat and pulled him back through the swinging doors.

A few minutes later the judges passed their score-cards under the door. Stanley ran over and greedily scanned the numbers. He let out a maniacal chuckle, but a sharp zap sent him spinning around with a grimace.

He threw the cards at Neil, scattering them on the counter. Neil gathered them up and saw the truth. Stanley and DBC were ahead by two points. He had lost round one. He'd never had that happen before. He didn't like it. He could feel his chest begin to heave.

"Now," Stanley said with a smile, "let's see what dish you've come up with."

Chapter Fourteen

Fuel and Engines

Larry sat in his favorite booth at the coffee shop, sipping a perfectly warm and silky, not hot and foamy, cappuccino. The wonderful drink only distracted him for a moment, however, and he found himself staring at the door again. Down the street he knew Neil was fighting for his livelihood, if not his life, against a supercomputer . . . and a curse. Larry had told Neil he shouldn't walk into this duel alone.

"Why are you trusting this guy? He designs attack programs for the military for crying out loud! He sets up air-conditioning systems that explode!"

Neil hadn't even taken his eyes off the onions he was dicing. "I don't trust him, but if he simply wanted to destroy the restaurant, or me, he could have done that already. He wants more. He wants to beat me to show that he's the best, or that DBC is. And he'll want witnesses. I can almost bet you that his judges will be top critics or chefs. And don't stress. I'm going to win. I've beaten him before. Now go get a coffee, or twenty."

Larry had to admit that was a good suggestion, but he still wasn't happy. Neil had ordered him out of the kitchen and told him to keep quiet about the details of the duel. No cops. No Isabella. No Angel. So Larry sat and stewed—and drank coffee—and prayed he didn't hear any explosions.

I might as well be useful, he thought. Larry pulled out the recipe book and his notes. If Neil wouldn't let him help in the kitchen he'd do his best to help crack whatever code was hidden inside. Of course, Neil needed a particular recipe from the book for the duel, but Larry had already worked out that problem.

Larry flipped through his notes. He'd tried to do some investigating into his family history. But, according to his research, there was no mention of the Flambés anywhere. This struck him as extremely odd. No family history at all? It was like someone had erased all trace. If these "F's" were all such great chefs, why weren't there any records of their existence?

Larry thought back to his own house. There were no family photos, no family heirlooms . . . nothing. He'd even (gasp) been able to corner his parents for a few minutes, but even they didn't seem to know where the family had come from. And they certainly didn't know if there were any great chefs in the Flambé line.

"We never cooked at home," his dad had said, not looking up from his research into a new prescription drug for treating foot fungus. "Dad always told us food was just like gas in a car . . . fuel. Neil's dad couldn't even boil water. And we are still far too busy to waste time in the kitchen . . . or to answer any more questions."

"And as for family history," his mother added. "Who cares? We look to the future, not the past. We're too busy to bother with family trees or cooking. That's what our parents always told us—'Work, work, work.' By the way, are you at all close to getting a real job? Your father and I could put in a word at Samson Laboratories. . . ."

Larry didn't recall the rest of the conversation. He'd heard variations on it for years anyway.

So his family had no traceable history or love of cooking, yet Neil's theory was that this book in front of him traced the Flambé love of food for more than ten centuries.

"That is what we call a conundrum," Larry said out loud to his coffee. "And if these are all Flambés, then what do the dates and symbols mean?"

Larry decided to take a different tack. He pulled out his smart phone. Larry had bought the phone after their recent trip to Mexico City—"It should save me lugging all those books around." Neil had a new phone as well, so he could download all the cooking apps. Both were state-of-the-art.

Larry typed in the name Valette.

Thousands of matches appeared, most having to do with a small manufacturing firm in Malta. It made kitchen equipment. Hmmmm. That was sort of promising, but there didn't seem to be any direct ties to DBC or the Flambés.

He tried "Valette Food Cordon Bleu." That didn't narrow things down as much as he'd hoped, but one of the pages did mention an order of knights that had once fought in the Crusades. A certain Jean Valette had been a member of the order, and had been imprisoned for a while, and had then started the company. "Interesting, interesting," Larry said to the coffee. Was there a Flambé fighting alongside back in the good old days of war and mayhem?

Larry tried typing in everything he could think of about the past few days.

"Valette Food Cordon Bleu Circle and Cross Flambé Curse Crusades Duels Notebooks DBC."

He hit enter. Only one entry popped up.

The link to the page read, "If you have found this page, the curse has returned. The key to the code is 1291. Do not go to Paris."

Larry quickly jotted down the information and then clicked on the link. There was no web page. Error 404 flashed on his screen. "What the—?" He typed in the same search parameters and clicked enter.

His screen read. "Sorry, there were no matches." He tried to refresh the page. It had disappeared. He hit the back button, no page. Larry let out a low whistle. Things were already weird, but this was getting creepy.

"All right, so don't go to Paris, 1291. I can barely afford to go home," he said, laughing. "So that's an easy warning to heed. What the heck is so significant about 1291? Maybe it's the cost of a flight to Paris? Or a date? Valette was jailed around that time." Larry quickly accessed his account at the library and downloaded some books about the Crusades. The shortest one was four hundred pages. "Whew, I'm going to need more coffee."

Chapter Fifteen

Canada Goosed

Neil walked over to his cooler. DBC was ahead? AHEAD? That meant that he, Neil Flambé, was BEHIND? His nose began to throb again, and so did his heart. He was up against it big-time. Neil had no intention of never cooking again—Picón had no way of enforcing that—but Neil knew if he lost the duel he would lose his restaurant, his reputation, and what remained of his confidence. Larry would have to find new work. Angel might never speak to him again. Isabella? She'd called him a bambino and Neil hadn't done anything to change her mind about that.

If Picón hadn't pulled that last-second trick with the recipe rule, Neil would be ahead, but he couldn't believe how close the voting had been regardless. The sense of panic began to grip his chest. He had to suppress it.

It was time for his final gambit. Neil lifted the lid off the cooler, revealing two perfectly plucked Canada geese. He lifted them by the necks and held them proudly in the air.

"Time for dish number two," he said.

"You must be joking," Picón scoffed. "Those are just feathered rats!"

"You told me to pick the ingredients for one dish. I've picked Canada geese, freshly plucked off one of the city's finest golf courses not more than a few hours ago." Neil was no hunter. But Larry had a friend who called herself The Forager, who had an incredible ability to find all sorts of rare herbs and vegetables growing in the fertile soil of the lower mainland—and sometimes proteins; pheasant, pigeon, that sort of thing.

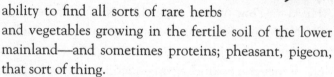

When Neil and Larry had tracked her down the night before under the Burrard Street Bridge, she'd been a little surprised at the request—usually the Flambés came to her for more mainstream things like truffles—but she'd delivered.

Picón gritted his teeth. The zapping sounds grew more frequent. "No one wants . . . to . . . eat . . . those . . . things!"

Neil thrust one of the geese onto Picón's chopping block. "You're lucky. I already handled the tough work of cleaning them. Did you know the Canada goose poops every ten seconds, on average?" This was a tidbit Larry had shared with him. He didn't like the image any more than Picón but he hoped it unnerved him a little. "Start cooking. You have an hour."

"Fine." Zap. "We cook this rubbish, but what is the recipe?"

"No recipe."

"What do you mean 'no recipe'? There has to be a recipe."

"Great chefs don't need recipes. You now have fifty-nine minutes to make three dishes from that one goose." Neil turned back to his own cutting board and began separating the goose into its various parts.

He heard another series of zaps and watched as Picón flew toward his cutting board, his head and neck twitching as if he were being electrocuted. "I don't know, my child," Picón was whispering into his chest. "Look for recipes for normal goose, or maybe duck. We'll use those."

Neil smiled. Canada geese were more infamous than famous—better known for finding their way inside jet engines than onto dinner plates. One big reason for this is that they don't taste anything like a normal goose. You have to prepare them in a very particular way or end up with something resembling either burned shoe leather or raw fish eyes.

Even if DBC tried to match the spices, there was no way he'd be able to cut and prepare the meat as well as Neil.

And Neil wasn't being totally honest when he said there was no recipe. He discreetly ran his finger along his collar. If Picón looked over he would think Neil was just dealing with his nerves, or the heat, but Neil was looking down his front at the list of ingredients Larry had copied from the Flambé recipe book onto Neil's very own me-shirt. This was exactly the sort of food his ancestors had been forced to cook, and their experience was now going to give him the advantage he needed.

He was prepping his goose for sausage, seared breast meat, and a goose-broth–infused garlic mashed potatoes with grilled root vegetables. Neil began by putting the tougher dark meats through a grinder, creating a hash that he quickly sautéed in his frying pan with spices—his shirt told him to use something called "the grains of paradise," a peppery spice Larry said was common in the middle ages. It was also a spice Neil was sure Stanley and DBC didn't have in their pantry or their database. DBC might smell it, but couldn't replicate it.

Picón was standing in front of his bird, trying to figure out what the heck to do with it. "That's a recipe for duck," he whispered to his chest. "It will have to do," said the electronic voice.

"It will have to do" was music to Neil's ears. He smiled as he prepped the neck of the goose as a sausage casing, and soaked the breasts in brine—a combination of salt, sugar, and water. He took the cooked dark meat and spices and stuffed them into the casing, tied the ends, and then placed the sausage in the oven to quick-cure.

He took the remaining edible bits of the bird and threw them in a pressure cooker with some onion, garlic, and another spice the book had recommended called cubeb—a spice Marco Polo had even written about in his travels. "The official travels," Larry had pointed out, remembering their nasty encounter with the secret diary of Marco Polo a few months before. "So this spice is legit, not poisonous . . . I think."

Picón and DBC seemed to be getting into heated arguments about spices, cooking times, methodology, and each other. Picón started sweating, not a great idea when you're hooked up to a sophisticated electronic game console. The electric zaps seemed to be causing him increasing pain and his head frequently hung limp on his shoulder while DBC kept his arms chopping, sautéing, and seasoning.

In the final few minutes, Neil quickly pan-seared his goose breasts, used the rich meaty broth to make his mashed potatoes, and then cut up and pan-fried the sausage.

Picón and DBC had done their best to turn the goose into something resembling a Thanksgiving turkey. The result, an unevenly cooked series of tough breast cutlets and nearly raw curried goose thighs, was not what they were hoping for. They knew it, and Neil knew it. He smiled.

The judges were merely afterthoughts for Neil now. A wave of relief poured over him. He wouldn't have to lose the restaurant, the curse was defeated. He wasn't sure how Stanley had found out about the whole curse thing, but now he was about to break it.

As Neil placed his dishes before the judges, he told them they should score the meal out of ten for "taste, texture, and originality." Picón fidgeted and twitched as the judges devoured Neil's succulent game, and left DBC's largely untouched. A long loud zap sent Picón running back through the kitchen doors. Neil followed at his own confident pace.

He pushed open the doors. Stanley Picón was standing next to the sink, shaking with rage and second-degree electrocution burns. He moaned, "No, no, no . . . not again. It's impossible."

The judges slid their score cards under the kitchen door, confirming Neil's handy victory.

Then everything went crazy.

Picón gripped the steel counter. Blue sparks flew from where his fingers touched the metal. He began to shake uncontrollably.

Neil walked up to him and pointed a finger in his face. "You and that glorified cassette deck owe me some money." Picón's eyes began to bug out, and he struggled to look at Neil. His teeth remained clenched as he said, "It has already been transferred to your account."

"No way, not good enough. Cough it up in cash."

Picón did cough, and a slit opened on the front of his chest. Hundred-dollar bills began pouring out like an ATM machine, flying onto the floor and counter as Picón's body lurched and swung.

Neil scooped up the bills, but he wasn't done. "Good. And now that I've won, I don't ever want to hear anything more about a curse. No more threats to my friends or family. Do you understand?"

Picón's hair began to smell faintly of smoke. "Curse? What are you talking about?"

"Don't lie to me!" Neil yelled. He angrily grabbed Stanley's shoulder to swing him around. A loud zap like lightning crackled in his ears as the shock sent Neil flying across the kitchen floor, slamming him into the far wall. The brief interruption of the current also allowed Picón to release his grip on the counter.

"You tried to kill me!" Picón screamed. Neil looked up, but Picón wasn't yelling at him, he was looking down at the device on his chest. "I am not happy." Then he ran out the kitchen doors into the dining room.

Neil shook his head and struggled to stand up. He stumbled to follow. He couldn't let Picón get away. He needed more answers. He swung open the doors and lurched into the dining room. The judges had disappeared, probably to find some dessert joint to confab about their strange evening of fine dining.

Picón wasn't in the dining room either. Neil looked outside, where Picón was crawling along the sidewalk toward a large white van. He seemed to be fighting himself, frequently grabbing at his chest while getting punched in the head by his own hand.

Neil marched up beside him just as he got to his knees and reached up to open the door. The inside was glowing, as if Christmas tree lights were going on and off.

"Tell me about the curse!" Neil yelled, yanking on Picón's collar and doing his best to avoid the coils and wires.

"I don't know anything about a curse. I told you. I was only a subcontractor."

"I thought that was a joke about the air-conditioning system," Neil said, tightening his grip.

"I was offered money to defeat you in a duel at Chez Flambé. I assured him I could. Now he's going to come for me." Picón's eyes grew wide with panic.

"Him? Him who?"

"You're saying too much," said an electronic voice from inside the van. Suddenly, Stanley's right arm jerked up to his throat and began strangling him. "You're compromising the mission."

"No, DBC. The mission is OVER. We lost AGAIN," Picón squeaked.

His hand released his throat and grabbed the steering wheel, pulling him inside the van, kicking and screaming. "This loss was your fault," said the voice, with what Neil was sure was a tinge of anger and possibly fear.

"We can try again. We must try again!" Picón yelled.

"NO. You are too weak! Humans are too weak!" screamed DBC. "Error, error . . ." Acrid black smoke began to fill the cabin of the van. Neil could hear sparks and short circuits, and an ominous glow illuminated the windows.

"We are both weak. We must both pay for this failure," said DBC, his voice suddenly sounding eerily calm.

Picón's left arm grabbed him by the throat. His right arm turned the ignition.

"Stanley. Who were you working for?" Neil yelled, holding the door open.

"I . . . don't . . . know . . . name . . . Paris . . . 1291 . . ."
He passed out.

"DBC. Who were you working for?" Neil screamed into the back of the van.

DBC didn't answer, but began to sing, *"Non, je ne regrette rien."*

There was a zap and Picón's left arm lashed out, knocking Neil back onto the sidewalk. Another zap and the door slammed and Picón's leg floored the gas. The van sped off, fire and smoke now pouring out of the doors and windows.

Neil watched as it sped around the corner.

"Paris, 1291," Neil said. He had a sudden flash of the cross and circle in his mind. Had he seen it somewhere in Paris?

He stood up and walked back into the restaurant just as the can of tuna in his fridge exploded, sending the door flying off its hinges and through the kitchen doors into the dining room. Chairs, tables, and glassware shattered, filling the entire room with debris right in front of Neil's eyes.

He gripped the door handle so hard he thought it would break. He stood there for what seemed like an eternity. The curse wasn't over. But it would be.

It was time to end this stupidity. Neil had gained a lot tonight. He had some money. He knew he could cook again. He also knew someone was still out to get him, and he was darned if he was going to put off that battle any longer. He slammed the door shut. The glass cracked. Neil rubbed his temples, then ran to hail a cab.

Chapter Sixteen

Not-So-Ancient History

Larry dialed the number for the Medieval History department at UBC. "If you know the extension . . ." Larry cut off the recorded message by hitting the numbers 1066. Four cups of coffee and some seriously deep reading had yielded some possible leads, but Larry needed to call in an expert to speed things up. Luckily for the Flambés, Larry personally knew the world expert on the Crusades.

"Adrianne Tortosa here," answered a sultry voice on the other end.

Larry smiled. Even the sound of her voice was beautiful. He and Adrianne shared a love of dates. Of course, hers were medieval, his were romantic.

"*Salve, amica, quid novis?*" Larry said

"*Salve* yourself, you Latin loser."

The call was not starting off quite the way Larry had hoped. "Wait a minute. You and I were supposed to go to that Fra Angelico exhibit last week, weren't we?" Larry realized sheepishly.

The *grrrr* on the other end of the line confirmed it. Ever since he'd sold the Harley, Larry had been finding it much harder to juggle his various "engagements." Showing up at a big art exhibit on a bicycle just wasn't cool, Neil was living proof of that . . . but it meant stuff was slipping through the cracks in his busy schedule. Neil cracking up just made it all worse.

"Look, I'm sorry about that. It's been really nuts at the restaurant lately," Larry said.

"Nuts? Is that another of your cooking jokes?"

"You don't know the half of it." Larry chuckled. The sound of his laugh softened her tone a bit. Everyone found it hard to stay mad at Larry—except, of course, Neil.

"So . . . why the call all of a sudden?"

"Well, I called to apologize for missing the exhibit, of course!"

Adrianne paused. "And?"

". . . And, yes, I need some help with some history stuff—1291 in particular."

"Hmm. Doesn't 1291 mean anything to you?" she said.

"I know it's the last four digits of Stephanie Pitt's cell phone number," Larry said, and immediately smacked himself on the head.

"Stephanie who?"

"Um, she's an old lady who teaches piano down at the conservatory." Larry didn't specify how old and he hoped Adrianne wouldn't ask.

"Well, 1291 was when the last real Crusade ended," Adrianne said as Larry breathed a sigh of relief. "The last Christian forces had been thrown out of the Holy Land and retreated to a city on the coast. There was a long siege and the knights eventually surrendered. Most spent the rest of their lives in prison."

Larry was thinking. "Was there anything particularly weird about this siege?"

"It was pretty straightforward, although historically significant, in that it effectively ended any Crusader presence in the Middle East."

"So 1291 was the end of the Crusades? Do you happen to know anything about food or cooks from that time?"

"The key to any siege is denying food to the enemy."

"Yeah, that's not exactly the sort of thing I mean."

"Wait a minute," Adrianne said. "This is tweaking something. I was at a conference in England last year. This professor was presenting a talk on cooking and the Victorian Ages. He was really boring. . . ."

"Not as good a teacher as you are, obviously."

"Flattery will get you everywhere. But one of the details was interesting. He'd found a reference to a medieval siege in a note someone had tucked into one of the cookbooks."

"Right up your alley."

"Exactly. He wasn't too interested in it, so I asked him if I could have it for my research. He sold it to me."

"Okay! I knew you'd come through."

"More flattery. Keep it up. The note was in French. The weird thing is that the parchment was very old but the writing was concurrent with the cookbook, probably late 1800s. I haven't really looked at it closely but I have it here somewhere. . . ." Larry could hear her digging through some papers.

"This cookbook didn't happen to belong to anyone named Flambé, did it?"

"No, it was Herringbone or Smeltington or something like that. Not a French name. Ah. Here's the note." She was silent for a minute or so.

"Adrianne, you still there?"

"Interesting," she said.

"What?"

"Well, this talks about a siege around the same time, 1291, but with some minor order of knights. These knights, the order of the *orbus caeruleum* . . ."

"Blue circle?"

"Yes. I've never heard of them before. They were besieg-
ing a walled city near Acre. The Turks and one of their chief leaders were trapped inside. It looks like the knights were starving them out."

"Nasty things, these sieges."

"Yes, and this one was particularly nasty. The knights, I guess recognizing that they were desperately clinging to the Holy Land, had pulled out all the stops and were more cruel than usual. They'd made a deal to let the women and children out, and then slaughtered them at the gates."

"Nice. So why did me mentioning 'food' click something for you?"

"This siege ended strangely. One day the Turks were ready to surrender and the next day they retracted the agreement and launched a counterattack. If they'd surrendered, it would have freed the knights to join the main force."

"It also would have turned a small army of Turks into prisoners."

"Exactly, eliminating a big threat to the Crusaders, and maybe giving them a chance to retake the Holy Land."

"So what happened?"

"Someone had used a catapult to fire the knights' food supply over the walls. The Turks gained strength and confidence, and then fought back."

"Does it say who?"

"Not on this note. It does mention one other thing, though. The leader of this group of knights was particularly nasty, apparently. His name was Jean Valette."

Larry almost leaped out of his chair. "Holy mackerel. Listen, Adrianne, I need you to do one more thing for me."

"Okay."

"I need you to soak that piece of paper in water."

"What? You're kidding. This cost me a hundred bucks!"

"No, I'm really not kidding . . . this time. I'll pay you back."

Adrianne scoffed.

"Okay, we'll work out a barter system later, but please hurry," Larry said.

"Okay, I have a vase of flowers here somewhere . . . sent to me by someone else!"

Larry heard the sound of something being dunked. There was a pause.

"Oh, my goodness," she said.

"What's there?"

"It says the name Flambé and the date 1291."

"And there's a symbol?"

"Yes, a cross and circle. Amazing."

Larry stood up and headed for the café door. "Adrianne, thanks. *Amo te, Sabidi*. I gotta run and tell Neil."

"Wait, one more thing," Adrianne said. "How old is this piano teacher?"

A few minutes later Larry was standing in front of the disaster area that was supposed to be Chez Flambé. The dining room looked like a bomb had gone off. The kitchen doors were off their hinges and the fridge door had somehow lodged itself halfway through the dining room wall.

I don't think duct tape is going to fix it this time, Larry thought. He tried the front door. It was open. He searched inside, stepping over the dusty remnants of the new restaurant chairs and tables. He picked up an underdone goose drumstick. It was still slightly warm.

"Neil!" Larry yelled. "Neil, if you're hiding I need to talk to you. I know why there's a curse on us, Neil! And for some reason we can't go to Paris."

Just then Larry's phone beeped.

He looked down at the text message on the screen.

Neil here. DBC defeated. Off to find his boss. Clean the mess.

Larry stared at the words and frowned. "Why does he never say please?"

Chapter Seventeen

Pâté Cake, Pâté Cake, Baker Man

Neil Flambé knew his way around Paris. The city was always alive in his memory and his imagination. Anyone who loves food has visited Paris and can feel the gastronomic delight in the air the second they step foot out of the metro.

Neil did just that, stepping out of the Cité metro

station in the cool of the morning, the chapels and castles of the ancient French aristocracy glowing like gold in the rising sunlight. Rising above it all, the great cathedral of Notre Dame, glistening white, the bells ringing.

Neil wasn't here for the scenery, however, but to solve a mystery. Unfortunately, he had no idea what to do next. The moment he'd taken his seat on the flight, he'd realized how crazy he was being. He felt he needed to be a little crazy, though. Until a few hours before, Neil had assumed Picón and DBC had been the masterminds behind the curse—but Picón seemed genuinely ignorant of the tampered silverware and the Carrion restaurant. So who was DBC working for?

Picón had said the words "Paris" and "1291." Paris was easy to figure out. But 1291? What the heck did 1291 even mean? Was it a code? A street address? Not likely. Hardly any Paris street numbers went that high. A date? He'd decided it might be, so he'd headed straight to the oldest part of town, the heart of the city. It occurred to Neil that this was a bit of a wild goose chase. But he was going to chase this particular goose down and cook it to death.

Neil hadn't forgotten the note warning him to stay away from Paris. Maybe, though, it had been left by DBC's boss to make sure Neil didn't go to Paris. Sure, some crazy knife-wielding chef might be waiting there, ready to jump out at him, but that wasn't anything new.

His stomach rumbled. He had been in such a rush he had neglected to pack any food in his tiny backpack. All he had were his passport, a couple pairs of socks and underwear, and a few shirts. The food on the plane, a last-minute charter with a group of traveling vegan acrobats, had been a choice of what looked like rubbery tofu or tofu-y rubber—in short, inedible. He was starving.

Neil had a few hundred euros in his pocket. And he knew exactly where he needed to go: Hugo Victoire's Lunchback Café. It wasn't just the food that was amazing there—something was nagging at Neil, a hint of a memory. When Picón mentioned Paris, Neil remembered the symbol of the circle and cross. It was there somewhere, and he'd seen it before. Neil couldn't quite remember exactly where he'd seen it, but when he thought of Hugo, an image of the symbol flickered in his mind.

Neil hoped it was open. There was only one way to find out.

Neil walked straight toward Notre Dame Cathedral, but instead of heading into the church, he made an abrupt right turn and headed for the entrance to the public washrooms. He stopped and sniffed the air.

He smiled. Mixed in with the smell of cleaning fluids and . . . other things, was the unmistakable aroma of freshly, perfectly baked croissants. Neil slipped down the stairs. At the bottom sat an old woman, knitting. At her feet were a bottle of cleaning fluid, a towel, and a small copper pot for tips. To her right a bank of turnstiles led to the washrooms. To her left was a closet door.

Neil took out a five euro note and folded it in the shape of flower, like the napkins at Chez Flambé. He handed the flower to the woman. She lifted an eye and stared suspiciously at the young chef. "*Mot de passe?*" she said grumpily.

"Quasimodo," Neil said. He hoped it was still the right password—it had been a while since he'd been here.

A young couple skipped down the stairs and dropped a few coins in the copper tin then went through the turnstiles, kissing before they went to their separate bathrooms. Neil felt strange watching them. Parisians were so demonstrative. He couldn't imagine kissing Isabella before heading to the bathroom.

As soon as they were gone the old woman looked all around and, when she was sure they were alone, clicked a button somewhere on the leg of her chair and nodded toward the closet door, which now opened a crack.

Neil hurried through. The door clicked shut behind him and threw him into darkness. He blinked a few times until his eyes adjusted to the gloom. A soft glow shone from somewhere below. He walked down the stone hallway until he reached the top of an iron spiral staircase, all the while the smell of the baking growing more intense and more complex. There was also the murmur of people talking.

Neil stepped carefully down the stairs, down another short hallway, and finally through a tiny arched doorway. He walked into a large domed room, constructed of smooth-cut stone. Enormous wooden beams crossed from wall to wall above, keeping the stone from collapsing under the weight of the Seine. Neil couldn't hear water, but he knew the river was right above them.

A dozen or so tables were set up on the stone floor. Candelabras sent a dim light through the room. This was a place to eat great food, with a side dish of privacy. Neil walked toward the kitchen, passing tables of people devouring delicately flaky pastries and steaming milky coffee. Neil was fairly certain he recognized the French president and a woman who wasn't his wife, seated in a corner. Two more steps and he passed a table with two actors he was sure were in a movie he'd seen on a flight once, something to do with a kidnapped French king and some guys in big feathered hats. Neil mostly remembered the food from the movie's wedding feast scene. At another table, two women in large black trench coats were exchanging what looked like money and a briefcase of documents.

The aroma of rising dough grew stronger with each step.

"Manna from heaven," Neil said as he swung open the kitchen doors and walked through.

A short man with a tiny white mustache and goatee was leaning over a kitchen counter, adding a large slab of butter to a thin layer of pastry dough. He was concentrating so hard that he didn't notice Neil walk in. Neil watched as he first pounded the two together with a rolling pin and then spread the dough thinly, over and over again, until the butter and dough became one. Then he covered the dough and placed it into a fridge.

The man took another rack of dough out, already rolled and now chilled, and walked back to the counter. He cut the dough into small squares. Then he rolled each square into small crescents, and let them sit. Neil

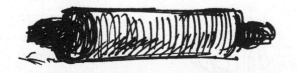

couldn't resist a huge smile. He was watching a master at work, like a great ballet dancer on a stage.

Then the man walked over to another section of the counter where yet another selection of pre-rolled crescents sat rising. One final brush with egg white on the top of each, and then they were placed onto a baking sheet and into the oven.

With a sigh the man wiped his hands on his apron and then turned around and with a start, finally noticed the young red-headed chef at his kitchen door. A huge smile spread across his face. "Neil? Neil Flambé! Here in Paris?"

"And famished, Hugo. Can you believe the cardboard they try to pass off as airplane food?"

"You are too young to remember the days when flying meant something, when Cordon Bleu–trained chefs prepared salmon mousse in the aisles as you watched. Ah, it was *magnifique*!"

"These days it's more like salmon mouse, if you're lucky. I wasn't," Neil scoffed.

"Ah, my talented young friend, it has been far too long. What can I get you?"

"As if you don't know."

Hugo smiled. "Croissants."

"*Mais oui.* Fresh, Hugo-made croissants." Neil wished Larry and Isabella had been there to see this—a chef who didn't want to kill Neil, or beat him in a duel, or run him out of business. Neil didn't ever admit anyone was a better chef than he was, but a rare few were better at specific things. Hugo

was the greatest pastry chef Neil had
ever met. This, of course, was not
something he would say publicly.

He did once admit it to Hugo,
who had responded by saying
Neil was almost as good, and
certainly would be if he'd
concentrated on croissants
alone. Neil respectfully agreed.
Of course, Hugo's croissants had
helped Neil win a sandwich-themed
duel a few years before. Neil had prepared a chicken in Dijon and mushroom sauce,
and Hugo's pastry had perfectly enclosed the chicken in
buttery silkiness. Neil called it his *croque mystique*.

A waiter shuffled into the kitchen with an armful of
orders. "That group of rich schoolgirls has arrived and
the nun has promised them all croissants."

Hugo motioned to Neil to have a seat. "We will talk
in a minute, but I must attend to the customers, you
understand."

Neil nodded. "Need any help?" he said, slipping off
his backpack.

Hugo smiled. "Always a chef. *Non, mon ami.* You rest
after your flight. Please, *s'il vous plait*, take a seat and
relax. A fresh batch will be out soon. And I still have a
tiny *morceau* of that amazing summer berry jam you
taught me how to make. The president ordered it, but I
will send him some marmalade . . . along with my regrets."

Neil sat on a stool and ate and watched Hugo
work—and made more than a few mental notes on how

he could make better croissants when he got back to Chez Flambé.

Neil and Hugo grabbed two ancient-looking wooden stools and sat down at the kitchen counters. "The dining room is for mere mortals, not gods. We shall sit in the kitchen," Hugo said. The last customers had gone back to their important—or at least affluent—lives in the city above.

"What brings you to Paris? Another duel? I thought you were scaling back on those."

"It's not a duel—at least not that I'm aware of," Neil said. "It's a curse."

He expected Hugo to be taken aback, or to laugh, but insd he stared straight into Neil's eyes. "So, it's true. You poor *miserable*."

"You know about the curse?"

Hugo sat back and rubbed his beard. "Not the details, but there are whispers, legends. There are many chefs— and others who care about food—who follow your progress from afar, you know. You show such . . . promise. But I have heard it said that you are losing your skills and that you may lose your restaurant."

"I was losing everything." Neil frowned. "But it wasn't me and it wasn't any stupid supernatural curse. It was some nutball with an egotistical calculator and some bad silverware."

"So if you have solved the problem, why are you in Paris?"

"The nutball I mentioned . . . he said he was working for someone he met here in Paris."

"Did he say anything else?"

"He mentioned a number. I can't figure out what it means. 1291."

Hugo's eyes grew wide. "1291?"

Neil nodded.

Hugo walked over to his counter and grabbed a large silver spoon. Then he walked over to one of the large wooden beams that formed the top of the kitchen door. "Look here," he said.

Neil walked over. The wood looked very old, but otherwise unremarkable. He shrugged. "I don't see anything."

Hugo used the spoon to reflect the candlelight onto the wood. "How about now?"

Neil could see shadows where someone had carved the number 1291 and the symbol of the cross and circle.

"I knew I'd seen that here before!" Neil said. "But what is it and what is it doing here?"

"I have no idea." Hugo took down the spoon. "I don't know what it means. But I have thought about it much since I took over this rather unique place."

"Took over?"

"I did not build this bakery. I discovered it, hidden here in the sewers. It was clear that it had been a kitchen before. But who had created it?" He stared hard at Neil who simply shrugged. He wasn't quite sure what Hugo was getting at.

Hugo continued, never taking his eyes from Neil. "There is a legend of a great chef, a young boy who had dazzled the salons of Paris with his ability to cook. He was on his way to great things, amazing things. But he was cocky. He made many enemies, many powerful enemies. One day, he disappeared after a great fight, a duel. Half of a Paris arrondissement burned down that night."

"This was in 1291?"

"No," Hugo said. "This was in the 1800s. It was assumed that this chef had died in the fire. Bodies were found. He had no family. He was just a boy at the time, barely more than fifteen."

Neil felt the hairs rise on his neck. "Who was this chef?"

"His *nom de famille*, his last name, was Flambé."

Neil had been right. The book Angel had given him *was* a kind of family album, a chronicle of Flambé success . . . and failure. "But you said he had no family, and he died?"

Hugo lowered the spoon. "That was *la histoire*, the story. When we heard your name, we assumed it was a coincidence, perhaps an homage to this chef. But what if there is more to the story, hidden like this wonderful place? Perhaps this chef did not die. Perhaps he fled underground, literally, and perhaps he did go on to have a family. Perhaps he left this scratched number behind as a clue?"

"Possibly. But a clue of what?" Neil wondered.

Hugo paused and picked a delicate flake of pastry off his plate. "Neil. Do you know the history of the croissant?"

"Um, that's not my field, really. I let Larry worry about that historical stuff." All of a sudden Neil wished Larry were here. Larry was a crackerjack at this sort of thing.

"There's a story that *le croissant* was developed to

recognize a victory over the Turks. They fought under the symbol of the crescent moon, so . . . when you eat one you are celebrating the victory—that sort of thing."

"It's not true?" Neil asked, sensing skepticism in Hugo's tone.

Hugo pursed his lips. "Not factual. But it is true . . . in a way."

"Meaning what exactly?"

"I mean that it is a fact that the croissant has been around in different forms for centuries. But the truth is that it was eaten by certain knights to celebrate victories over the Turks . . . during the Crusades."

"Um, that's fascinating, but what does it have to do with the carving on your door?"

"These knights would adorn their croissants with a circle and cross. It was their brand, if you will, the symbol of their order."

Neil thought of the symbol he'd seen burned in his door, on his silverware, on the door here in Paris. Larry had wondered if it was a reference to the Cordon Bleu or to DBC. But Hugo was suggesting it was much older. Larry was right; Neil really needed to start paying closer attention to his history lessons.

"So, wait . . . you think this 1291 refers to a battle in the Crusades?"

"I am saying that the Crusades seem to be very important to your present quest."

"Did they ever cross out the symbol, like with an X or anything? Was that important?"

Hugo thought for a moment and then shrugged. "Not that I know of. The order disappeared, leaving

behind only a few recipes for croissants . . . and their specialty, hot crossed buns."

Neil stared at Hugo. "How do you know all this?"

Just then the waiter returned to the kitchen, looking agitated. "Sir, there is a delegation from Russia that has just arrived. They are demanding full privacy and fresh croissants."

Hugo stood up. "I'm afraid I must earn my own daily bread, young man. Please come back tomorrow and we will chat some more." He turned back to his dough, losing himself in the process of making his wonderful pastry.

"But how do you know this?" Neil asked again. Hugo was completely lost in his work.

The waiter tapped his foot, clearly waiting for Neil to leave so that the Russian delegation could make its incognito entrance.

"I can take a hint," Neil finally said, standing up. He reached down for his backpack. As he did he glanced down at Hugo's spoon, the one he had used to show Neil the 1291 date carved into the door frame. Discreetly, Neil flipped it over. Inscribed in the silver was the symbol of the circle and the cross.

Chapter Eighteen

Serving Notice

Sean Nakamura stood on the doorstep of Chez Flambé and surveyed the extensive damage. "Something happened here. I'm not sure it was anything criminal, but it was certainly destructive." He walked into the restaurant and gingerly stepped over the broken china that was scattered all over the dining room floor.

"Holy mackerel," Nakamura said, staring at the fridge door, embedded into the wall. "That's not going to be cheap to fix." Nakamura felt bad for Neil. He knew he was struggling against some big challenges right now, chief among them his rising debt.

Neil had donated a large chunk of money to an anti-poverty soup kitchen in Mexico City a few weeks before. Nakamura had thought it oddly out of character at the time, and now it seemed like bad business. "Always save for a rainy day, and it rains a lot in Vancouver," Sean's dad had always told him. Still, Nakamura had to applaud Neil's philanthropy . . . but it made it harder to imagine that Neil could bounce back from yet another expensive blow to his restaurant.

Nakamura looked at the health notice on the door. Chez Flambé could open again tomorrow, legally, but there was no way that was going to happen, unless Neil had some super cleaning power to go along with his super sense of smell.

Sean looked at the mess. Where was Neil anyway? And a second question struck him . . . where was Larry? Nakamura had received a call from Larry to come check out the restaurant. But there had been no one here when he'd arrived. Surveying the damage, he wasn't sure there was going to be anyone in Chez Flambé anytime soon other than the health department. In fact, maybe he should call the health department. Who knew what was in this dust? Probably asbestos, plaster, gypsum . . . certainly not salt and pepper.

He got out his phone. He started to dial the health department when the phone rang. Nakamura clicked answer and held the phone to his ear.

"Nakamura here."

"Hi, Inspector, it's Stromboli. We just fished a burned-out van out of False Creek. You'd better come take a look. There might be a body. We're not sure, but it looks like something big is inside the van."

"Anyone we know?"

"Too early to say, Inspector."

"I'll be right there," Nakamura said and hung up.

Nakamura had an odd sinking feeling. What if the

body was someone he knew? What if it was Neil? Or Larry? Stromboli wouldn't call him over unless he thought there might be a connection. Things were happening this past week that he couldn't pin down. They weren't crimes, more like odd occurrences. Nakamura didn't like that.

He got behind the wheel of his car, gunned the engine, turned on his siren and made a beeline for False Creek. Whatever was waiting for him there, he hoped it would help him get some sort of handle on what the heck was going on.

Neil needed to go to the bathroom. Hugo had served him more than a few glasses of his own special fizzy water with the croissants. Good thing the exit he took out of Hugo's café was right next to the bathroom. A peephole between the stacks of towels ensured that guests could emerge unseen. But Neil was certain the French president didn't exit this way, and the Russians certainly didn't come in this way. Where were the other entrances?

This and many other questions swirled in his head— but there were more immediate things that needed attention.

He started to rush past the attendant, who grabbed him by the arm.

"*Je m'excuse monsieur mais vous devez payer,*" she said.

"Pay? I already gave you five euros!" Neil said.

"*Payez!*" she insisted. Neil fumbled in his pocket for a few coins, all the while performing the universal *I need to go* dance. He dumped the coins in her copper pot and she let go of his arm. Neil practically sprinted inside and dashed into the nearest stall.

After a few seconds he noticed very quiet footsteps. He peered under the stall door. There was only one set of shoes, and they were facing his stall.

"Um, hello, *bonjour?*" Neil said.

"Neil Flambé. You were warned not to come to Paris."

It was Jean-Claude Chili!

"So you are the mastermind behind all this?" Neil said angrily.

"You are in great danger. Go home," Chili said. Then Neil saw the shoes turn and Chili walked out of the bathroom.

Neil stood up and fumbled for the door handle. He skidded past the sinks to the entrance, where the old woman stared at him like he was crazy. Neil realized his fly was still open. He turned around and yelled over his shoulder. "Where did that man go?"

"You were in the bathroom, *monsieur*, you tell me?" she said, without a trace of a smile.

He waved a twenty-euro note at the woman who scoffed and went back to her knitting. She either couldn't or wouldn't tell Neil anything.

Neil stared at the closet door. It was firmly shut. Neil walked over to the woman, and put his face close to hers and did his best to look threatening. "Listen here, madame, I'm looking for a short man with a mustache, and if I have to I'll rough you—"

Without a word the woman grabbed her cleaning bottle and, in mid-sentence, sprayed Neil full in the face.

The liquid burned his eyes and the inside of his nose and throat.

"Ahhhhh!" he yelled. Chili was suddenly the least of his worries. He needed to stop the burning. Neil tried to go back into the bathroom but the woman had locked the turnstiles. Neil cursed at her, then rushed up the stairs. He stumbled over to a nearby drinking fountain and splashed the water over his entire face. He'd had a few dangerous encounters with jalapenos and habanero peppers in the kitchen and this was almost as bad. The water did its trick and the pain subsided.

Neil took a deep breath, clutching the sides of the fountain so hard his knuckles hurt. Where did Chili go? He lifted his head and scanned the crowd. There was no sign of Chili anywhere. Neil stuck his still stinging nose in the air to see if he could smell which way Chili had gone. With a jolt Neil realized that he didn't actually know what Jean-Claude Chili smelled like. He'd never smelled anything on his clothes or his hair, or his . . . anything.

He lowered his nose. Chili was untraceable. How did he manage that? Neil needed to make a few calls. He had come to Paris on his own, on a kind of single-minded mission fueled by his own anger and desire to get to the bottom of this so-called curse.

He reached into his pocket. His cell phone was gone!

The bells of Notre Dame

began to toll the noon Angelus. The noise was so loud and sudden that it made Neil jump. He looked back at the cathedral. Everyone in the crowd was turned in his direction. . . . They seemed to be watching him. Was his fly still down? He stole a quick look. No. What was it?

Then he noticed the front of his jacket. It was covered in blood. He put his hand up to his nose, which was dripping. Neil squeezed his nostrils together. He didn't even know he was having a nosebleed. It must have been caused by the caustic cleaning fluid.

At the same time a scream from the crowd directed everyone's attention to the lavatory entrance, where Hugo Victoire was stumbling up the stairs, his apron stained red. He pointed at Neil and then collapsed in a heap. A few large men looked angrily at Neil and began to come toward him.

Neil fought the conflicting urges to faint and to help Hugo. He gave in to the even stronger urge to get somewhere else, fast.

Chapter Nineteen

A Rose by Any Other Price . . .

Isabella Tortellini threw a vial of rose oil across the room. It smashed on the opposite wall like a scented hand grenade. This was Isabella's private testing lab, a log cabin hidden in the woods near a ski hill on the North Shore Mountains, where she tried her ideas and worked out her formulas before sending them to the shop floor back in Italy for production and bottling. The latest tests were not going well. This was the second vial of aromatic oil Isabella had pitched already today.

"That rose oil wasn't cheap, you know," said Jones, who was gazing into a microscope at the one tiny bit of shrapnel he'd been able to salvage from the DBC canister explosion. So far it had yielded nothing of interest, other than that it had been painted metallic blue on the inside.

Isabella frowned at him. "It should have been cheap. It's fake, synthetic," she said. Isabella had many talents that made her perfumes world wide favorites, and she knew a real rose when she smelled one. "We will never order from that supplier again."

"You're not going to demand a refund?" Jones was a little taken aback. One of Isabella's skills was her business acumen. Isabella was not herself lately. She was distracted, frustrated, and a little angry.

"A refund of, what? A few hundred dollars? It is not worth my trouble."

Jones cocked an eyebrow at her, but was quiet. A few hundred dollars was not nothing.

Isabella slammed her fist down on the counter. "I detest fakes." Then she relaxed, holding her head in her hands. "I am so tired," she said. Normally, when the stress of work got her down, she would head to Chez Flambé for some interesting conversation and especially some amazing food. There were those short moments before the evening rush when she could sit in the kitchen and steal some time to just chat with Neil.

She knew that Jones, and as a result her mother, didn't understand what she saw in Neil. Certainly he wasn't the kindest, most handsome, or most articulate boy she had dated. But he had a fire inside him. Neil didn't see the world as a gray place where one simply lurched from day to day working at a desk or computer. He had ambition, but not just to be rich, or to drive fast cars and wear designer clothes. He had an ambition to make the world a more flavorful place. He saw the possibility of great beauty in something as humble as a potato, the soul-satisfying revelation possible in the simple combination of fresh herbs and a ripe heirloom tomato. He had an artist's soul. He knew that he and the world could be greater than they were. She knew that as well.

She also knew some of that inner fire was for her. She saw it in the extra care he took to prepare her dinner, in the kind and somewhat awkward way he smiled at her when she arrived at his back door to watch him prep. She could wait for that fiery young man to find his voice. She felt the same fire in her own heart, to make the world great, to be great, and maybe to help Neil be great as well.

But lately Neil was more like a wet blanket. His "poor me" act was getting tired. Was he never going to snap out of it? His rudeness was quickly becoming the only way he related to people—including his friends. Was Neil a fake? She was not going to be taken in by a rose that was really a dandelion with pretensions.

There was a knock at the door of the lab. "That's weird," Jones said, lifting his head from the microscope. He walked over to the door and peered through the peephole. A bike courier was already pedaling away. Jones opened the door and saw a package that read, "Delivery for Ms. Isabella Tortellini—up in the hills . . . somewhere." He slammed the door

and walked back into the lab. "I think we'll have to look for a new location. This one's been compromised." He peered out of the open window, like he was half expecting a sniper to open fire.

"Oh, don't be so dramatic," Isabella said, taking the envelope. The front had her name written in embossed purple ink. "This is very artistic," she said. She grabbed a silver knife and opened the envelope.

Inside was another golden paper, an embossed invitation. It looked like something Amber and Zoe would do, when they weren't waiting tables at Neil's restaurant. Isabella read it out loud: "'Miss Isabella Tortellini and Jones are invited to a grand dinner at Chez Flambé to celebrate the victory over Deep Blue Cheese and the end of the curse!'"

"So there was a duel?" Jones said. "That's why that weasel was testing meals out on us the other night."

Isabella nodded. The note was clear—Neil had most certainly dueled with the computer that had tried to kill her and Jones, and won. Still, she smiled. "So, Neil did fight back." Isabella was not a fan of duels, but she liked weak-kneed milquetoasts even less. "It says Neil will be serving an amazing meal tomorrow evening . . . no, the next evening, at Chez Flambé." Her eyes twinkled. "What will I wear? I need a new scent. Perhaps something that suggests blue." She got up and quickly began assembling different scents on her counter.

That's more like it, Jones thought. He didn't like Neil Flambé any more than he liked his cousin Larry, but he couldn't deny the effect he had on his young charge.

"And on second thought," she said. "Get me the number of that rose oil supplier. I'm going to give them a piece of my mind and—"

"—and they are going to give you a full refund," Jones finished her sentence, and smiled.

Chapter Twenty

Neil Actually Does Some Homework

Neil walked up to the imposing front door of the Bibliothèque Nationale. It was not the sort of place he usually frequented. He'd once visited, on a vacation in search of a recipe book by the great Roman chef Apicius (and in particular the recipe for pullum frontonianum, or chicken with a thick grape juice—amazing!), but the other million books and magazines held little or no interest.

Until now.

Hugo Victoire had said the number 1291 might have something do with the Crusades, and hot crossed buns . . . and croissants . . . and a fire back in the 1800s. It seemed like a bunch of crazy connections on the surface but Neil had seen enough crazy connections between food and history—not to mention crime—to know when to follow a lead.

Neil raised the collar

on his shirt as high as it would go and tucked as much of his hair as he could into his toque. He wasn't sure if this made him look less suspicious, or more.

Neil hoped Hugo was okay. He'd seen an ambulance rushing toward the cathedral as he'd rushed across the bridge and into the narrow alleys and laneways of the city's right bank. Once he'd lost himself in the crowd, he'd shoved his jacket into his backpack and grabbed the warmest shirt he could find. He'd have to find a new coat and a place to stay before the sun went down.

Maybe he'd try to sneak back to the restaurant later, when things had cooled down. Neil was confident he could prove his innocence to the police, if he could trust them, but he also knew blood tests don't happen as fast as TV shows would like to suggest, and he couldn't afford to be stuck in jail right now.

Neil needed to either find Picón's mysterious boss soon, or get back to Vancouver to salvage whatever was left of his life. And, he suddenly remembered, he was about to miss, and fail, a math test and yet another day of school. That would take some explaining to his principal. At least Billy Berger wouldn't get another crack at his head in gym class.

Neil walked inside and up to one of the library's computer terminals. He typed in the 1291, Crusades, food, curse, Flambé, fire, croissants, battle . . . every word he could think of. A small spinning hourglass appeared on the screen as the computer calculated the results. Neil looked around nervously. There was a stack of scrap paper and a pen next to the computer. Neil reached over and grabbed some.

People were looking at him. He hoped it was the toque. Could the police have posted wanted posters this quickly? He stared back at the screen.

One search result appeared, a book entitled *Tacuinum Sanitatis*. It was part of a special exhibition on *Gastronomie du Moyen Age*. Neil quickly wrote down the info. He clicked on the picture of the book to get a closer look, but the computer screen suddenly went black.

"I have had it with computers," Neil said, slapping the side of the screen. The screen blipped back on to the welcome page. Neil typed in the same search words, but this time no results appeared. "Weird. Just like Angel's answering machine. It's like it was never there." No matter, he had the file number for the book. He walked over to the information desk where a woman was filing ticket stubs into a slot in the desktop.

"*Pardon, madame. Mais je cherche l'exposition Gastronomie du—*"

"*Sous-sol, monsieur anglophone.* In the basement," the woman said, not looking up but gesturing toward the elevators. Neil was used to the so-called "customer service" here in Paris, but he found himself missing the twins, with their smiles and friendliness. Neil felt a twinge of guilt when he thought of his own tableside manner. Only a couple of days ago, Isabella had just about poked him in the eye because of his behavior. *One more thing to work on when I get back,* he thought.

He stepped into the elevator and pressed the button for the basement.

*　*　*

Angel Jícama put the final touches on his honey-pastry—Kab El Ghzal or "gazelle horns"—crescent-shaped almond cookies. He carefully dusted them with powdered sugar, then raised a cookie to his lips and took a tiny bite. It was delicious, almost perfect . . . almost. With the taste still on his tongue he sipped his mint tea. The flavors combined to create an almost completely new sensation. *Even closer to perfection,* he thought with a smile. *Perhaps it is time to mail the invitations.*

Angel only cooked one meal a year, practicing the dish over and over until it was as good as he could make it. Then he would name a date and hold a very expensive dinner. His chosen meal this year was a selection of Middle Eastern specialties, including everything from homemade bread and dates to couscous and spicy eggplant salad. "Some are from the so-called West, some from the Orient. I am trying to bring them all together on a table, in a way that the cultures have not found peace in real life," he had explained to Neil a few months before, when the idea first took root.

Angel wanted the guest list to reflect a similar hope. He was inviting people who might otherwise be considered adversaries to sit with him for at least one night. He was just finishing the addresses on invitations that would be mailed out in the morning to Israel, Syria, and Iran. The responses this year could take months to come back, so he was planning well ahead. He gently rubbed the melting sealing wax onto the back of the envelope and waited for it to cool.

He heard a slight *swish* sound from his living room. He put down the invitations and went to see what had arrived through his mail slot this time. A golden envelope sat on a Turkish carpet he had recently purchased for the dinner.

He opened the envelope and read the note. He smiled. "So, it appears I am not the only chef who thinks it is time for a very good meal. Well done, Neil." Then he made his way back to the kitchen to try out one more variation on his chicken tagine.

The elevator opened to a gloomy room. Dim lights illuminated a series of displays, many of them paintings of food of the Middle Ages, some recipes. At the very back, under a spotlight, there were a series of smaller books in glass cases.

Neil walked from display to display looking for the book. Finally, tucked into a corner at the very back of the room, he came to a clear glass display case. The words *"Tacuinum Sanitatis"* were written on a plaque on the wall. The case itself was empty, except for a small card. Neil leaned over for a closer look.

"*Cet article est en cours de réparation.* Removed for repairs."

Neil frowned. He needed to see that book. A security guard was standing in the doorway. Neil walked over to him. "Excuse me, sir. That book over there. I came all the way from . . . Manhattan to see it. It's for a homework assignment. Is there any way?"

The man shook his head. "I'm afraid it has been taken to the restoration room."

"Um, where is that?" Neil asked. The man pointed to a door next to a giant tapestry of a medieval feast. "But they will not let you in without proper credentials."

"Credentials," Neil repeated, considering. "*Merci.*" The man nodded and turned his attention back toward the displays. *The poor man must be bored out of his skull,* Neil thought. There was nobody else down here. At least the mean lady who was standing guard at Hugo's had her knitting to keep her occupied.

Neil walked toward the door. As he did, he pulled his notebook and a pen from out of his backpack. He felt an incredible urge to see the book and he was going to try a gambit.

He rapped on the door. After a few seconds it opened a crack and a small woman with gray hair appeared. She was wearing an odd pair of glasses with a normal lens on one side and a kind of telescope lens on the other.

"*Oui? Puis-je vous aider?*"

Neil said nothing. Instead he handed the woman the strip of paper with the book information. On the back he had drawn a circle and a cross. The woman flipped the glasses onto the top of her head. Her eyes grew wide as she stared at the paper. She quickly opened the door and waved Neil in. Then she poked her head out, looked around to make sure no one else was there, shut the door, and locked it.

She turned back toward Neil. "I hoped you would come, Neil Flambé."

* * *

Eric and Margaret Flambé sat down to their dinner of instant macaroni and cheese and microwaved hot dogs. They didn't speak to each other and barely registered the fact that it was a family meal. The food was bland and had a texture similar to Styrofoam, but that was fine with the Flambés. They were more interested in the papers they'd each brought home from work. The table was covered with documents and files and looked more like a desk than a dining room table.

Eric's father had always told him food was fuel, nothing more. "Flambés don't waste time cooking, or eating. There's too much work to do," was his constant refrain. He and Margaret had met in a supermarket when they were in college; both had been reaching for the last box of instant chick'n noodle soup.

Neither understood their son's obsession with food, or with working in the kitchen all hours of the day. They did understand hard work, however, and were glad that Neil had inherited their work ethic.

They loved Neil. They just kept their feelings to themselves. Eric's father constantly told him that their family had come from peasant stock—hard workers who toiled to make it in a harsh world. "Stop

moving forward, get emotional, or even stop for some frivolous treat like an éclair or gourmet hamburger, and you will be in serious danger of falling back into the pile of useless humanity. Keep moving, don't be weak, don't let down your guard."

There was a knock at the front door. Eric peered through the peephole.

A bike courier was standing there holding a golden envelope and a cell phone.

He was dressed like one of those hippy-dippys Neil was always buying goat cheese from at the farmer's market. Strike one.

Eric answered the door.

The courier smiled as the door swung open, revealing Eric, still dressed in his best suit and tie. "Yo! Business dude, got a package for ya!"

He sounded like Larry. Strike two. Eric grabbed the envelope.

"Do I need to sign for it?"

"No way, man, I don't enforce those fascist rules. Live and let live, that's my mott—"

Strike three. Eric slammed the door in his face. He turned back to the dinner table.

"Mail, dear?" Margaret asked, not looking up from her notes.

Eric sliced open the golden envelope. "Hmm, it's from Neil. He's throwing a reopening party for the restaurant. Nice paper, too. Things must be looking up for him." He paused, a small spark of emotion ignited in his heart. "He's never sent us a written invitation before. I think we should try to go."

"Fine. Let me move a few things around. Do you think Neil will cook us something we can recognize?"

They entered the details of the great Chez Flambé meal in their digital datebooks and within seconds they were both lost in their work.

Chapter Twenty-One

Knights Tempura

Neil stared at the restoration room. It was filled with high metal and wood shelves, packed with ancient sculptures and paintings and all sorts of ornamental stones. In between sat rows and rows of oak tables, all covered with ancient books. The woman scurried past Neil and stared intently at his red hair.

"Why did you say you hoped I'd come?" Neil said, involuntarily taking a step back.

"No time." She ran to the nearest table and pulled out a chair. "Hurry, the book is here."

Neil felt a tug of concern, but something in the woman's face told him to trust her. He walked over and sat down. The woman looked familiar, although Neil was certain he'd never met her before.

The woman went back to the locked door and put her ear to the gray metal.

Neil turned his attention to the book. There was a pair of white gloves on the table. Neil put them on and began turning the pages. It was a work of art, filled with gilded images of peasants making bread, royalty eating huge joints of meat. There were detailed pictures of herbs, fruit trees, hunting parties. There was also lots of Latin. Neil knew some words, and found himself lost in the gloriously rendered recipes and health advice.

The woman left the door and walked over to Neil. She leaned down next to him.

"It is beautiful, no?"

"Yes," Neil said, examining a page depicting dried raisins and honeyed pine nuts.

She bonked him on the head. "Stop looking at the food! I told you there was no time." Without putting on the gloves herself, she flipped to the back of the book. On the left page was a multicolored panel showing a siege. The people on top of the castle walls appeared emaciated, many resembling little more than walking skeletons. Some were just children. Neil looked at the knights gathered below, who seemed quite happy with this. Their cloaks were all emblazoned with the unmistakable symbol of a blue circle and cross. But there was one knight, almost hidden in the background, who did not look happy. He had flaming red hair, and was secretly loading a catapult with food.

On the right side the story continued in a series of smaller illustrations, laid out almost like a page in a comic book. The townspeople feasted on the food. In the next panel they attacked the knights, taking the leader prisoner. In the final scene the red-haired knight is seen riding off into the distance on a donkey, with a small satchel of what looked like gold.

Neil looked up. The woman was grinning and nodding her head.

"You don't expect to see an anti-Crusader illustration in a European manuscript, do you?"

Neil took her word for it and nodded back. "No, I don't, I guess. So what is it doing in here?"

"This is a copy of the original Arab book of wellness—brought back from the Holy Land by the crusaders. This copy was made around the year 1295."

"Not 1291, though," Neil said, trying to work out the connections.

She pointed at the left-hand page. "This was a battle that took place in 1291. For the Arabs who commissioned the book, it was significant."

"Why?"

"It was a turning point and they celebrated it. But all subsequent copies of the book were destroyed, or altered, to make sure this image was lost. But the copy you are reading was not destroyed. It lay hidden in a monastery for centuries. It was only discovered by accident."

"By whom?"

"By three people. My brother and I were the latest. We were on vacation years ago, in search of the perfect cheese. We knew of a cave in the north of Italy, run by a small order of monks. We drove there, and then hiked up a steep mountainside. We almost died on the treacherous path. But it was worth it."

"Good cheese?"

The woman smacked her lips. "The cheese was *magnifique*. We bought as much as we could risk carrying back down the mountainside. Then we began chatting with one of the brothers. He told us of their library and especially the ancient texts on food that they had helped preserve. The monk said they had only shown this book to one other person, a chef, more than one hundred years ago. That was the chef who had first taught them how to make their cheese even tastier."

"A genius, then," Neil said. "And he was the third person you mentioned had seen the book?"

"Yes. And he must have been very arrogant as well to suggest to a monk that he could make a better cheese. But he was right, and the monk rewarded him with a view at this book. They kept it hidden in the uppermost tower of the monastery. The kind brother led us to this same place and revealed this book. He was impressed with the recipes and so were we, but as we looked through the book I discovered also this page. This is the key to the curse. That knight who betrayed his order was—"

"—was named Flambé," Neil finished. Pieces were starting to come together in his head, but there were still so many unanswered questions, so many other threads to follow, so many other ingredients he needed to assemble to get to the bottom of all this.

The woman nodded. "*Oui*, Pierre Flambé. He betrayed his order in 1291."

"And he was cursed?"

She nodded again. "But not until later, when the surviving members of the order began seeking revenge. Your ancestor had made it back to Rome and was the Pope's personal chef, when—"

Just then there was a loud click as someone began to unlock the door to the restoration room.

The woman's eyes grew wide with panic. She slammed the book shut. "Hurry, *vite, vite,* go!"

The lock clicked and the handle on the door began to turn. As far as Neil knew, that door was the only way in or out, so he bravely took a step toward the door and got ready to fight his way through.

"No. Not that way. Over here, behind the bookcase."

The woman ushered Neil behind a tapestry and through a tiny steel door. He ducked and went through just as a loud crash came from the room behind. The woman shut the door and Neil was alone. He looked around. He was in a deserted alleyway filled with only a few trash cans and empty cardboard boxes.

He heard a click in the door he'd just passed through and decided he'd better hurry out of the alleyway and as far away from the library as he could.

Chapter Twenty-Two

A Sink Feeling

Sean Nakamura watched as the crane lifted the charred remains of a van out of the rocky bottom of False Creek. Witnesses said they'd seen the smoking vehicle flying toward the water, with an eerie blue light shining from the windows.

And the first reports said the van had come from Chez Flambé. Neil had been awfully cagey lately and Nakamura sensed there was more going on behind the scenes. This had all the hallmarks of a high-stakes duel—part of the underbelly of the culinary world that Sean usually ended up dealing with after somebody got cut, burned, or killed.

"Okay, Inspector, all clear," Stromboli called as the crane lowered the van onto the grass, water pouring out from every seam in the metal.

Nakamura walked over and started with a quick examination of the outside. It looked like a normal moving van, no windows at the back—exactly the kind of van that delivered linens and other supplies (not all legal) to restaurants all over the city. "The license plates

are still attached," Nakamura said, surprised.
"I figured this would be a stolen
vehicle."

"I'll get the station to trace them."
Stromboli wrote down the number
and walked away.

The doors were all locked.
Nakamura took his sleeve and rubbed
the water off the windows. He tried to
see inside, but the smoke had blackened
them. There were large dents and a few
holes in the body, but all bulged outward.
It looked like someone had been hammer-
ing against the sides of the van from inside.
*Maybe someone trying to punch their way out
before drowning?* Nakamura thought. He hoped he
was wrong. There didn't seem to be any other mark-
ings on the van. "I guess we need to crack this egg,"
Nakamura said.

Stromboli walked back, his brow furrowed and his
lips pursed.

"It's a rental." Stromboli shuffled his feet.

"Who rented it?"

"Don't know for sure. The guy at the agency says
someone paid cash."

"And? Don't they take any ID? Driver's license?

Stromboli avoided the Inspector's gaze. "Yup. He
says the driver's license belonged to someone named . . .
Larry Flambé."

Nakamura felt a knot forming in his stomach. "Let's
take a look inside," he said.

Stromboli nodded and grabbed a crowbar. He shoved it in the gap between the door and the frame of the van. The door gave a loud moan of protest. Nakamura looked at his own shoes and waited, bracing himself for the sight of a dead person, probably Larry, behind the wheel. The door creaked, then swung open. Nakamura took a deep breath and looked up. He exhaled. The cab of the van was empty. There was nobody at the wheel. He walked over and stuck his head inside. There was nobody in the back either. "That's a relief," he said.

He climbed inside. Scattered in the back of the van were the charred and twisted remains of what appeared to be a large computer. It looked like it had exploded.

"What was this, some kind of surveillance van?" Nakamura said, jumping out of the cab.

Just then a bicycle courier came up to the crime scene. "Wow, that's one pimped ride . . . for a mermaid!" The courier chuckled.

"There's nothing to see here," Stromboli said, forming a cross with his arms and shoving up against the courier.

"Hey, chill, Officer Bacon. I'm clean. I just have a delivery to some dude named Sean Nakamura."

Nakamura's ears perked up. "What kind of delivery?"

"I don't read the mail, man. That would be, like, illegal. It's just some goldy envelope thingy." The courier pulled the envelope out of his hand-stitched Guatemalan satchel bag and handed it to Nakamura.

Nakamura stared at his ornately written name as the courier got back on his bike and started to pedal away. It looked like the sort of the artwork the twins sometimes did for Neil's menus and daily specials board.

Nakamura had a few questions swirling in his head. "Hey, wait a second. How did you know I'd be here?"

"That's just what the guy on the phone said."

"What guy? When did he call?"

"Well, someone dropped these envelopes off yesterday at the office."

Nakamura raised an eyebrow. "Office?"

"Well, okay, my room down in the Ambassador Hotel."

Nakamura kept his eyebrow raised.

"All, right, fine. My tent down in Victory Park. Someone slid the envelopes and a huge wad of cash through the front zipper. I have a sign on my bike that says 'courier for hire' so I guess they found me that way. There was also a cell phone inside and a note saying a guy would call me and tell me where to deliver the packages."

"When did he call to say I'd be here?"

"About thirty minutes ago." The courier pulled out the cell phone and showed it to Nakamura. The number was unlisted.

"What did he sound like?"

"I didn't catch his name, sounded a bit like me, though . . . you know, handsome, intelligent!"

"I think I'll keep this phone," Nakamura said. "I want to take a closer look."

"Suit yourself." The courier shrugged. "Yours was the last envelope anyway. I gotta get back to work." He pedaled off.

Nakamura opened the letter and read the details of the invitation. "Looks like we're all getting a great meal tomorrow to celebrate the Nose's reopening. Just like the Nose to make a splash—" He stopped and looked at the watery van. "Splash," he repeated. Something wasn't sitting right about this whole thing. Yes, Neil could legally reopen the restaurant tomorrow, but Nakamura had just been there and seen the destruction. There was no way Neil was hosting a dinner party in twenty-four hours. Maybe Neil had arranged to have the invitations sent out before whatever happened had happened? But the courier had said someone had called him thirty minutes ago.

Nakamura looked at the courier's phone. He scrolled back to all the calls he'd received. There were four or five, all unlisted numbers. Suddenly the phone buzzed. It was a new text message:

"See you all tomorrow. Neil."

"Neil? How the heck would he know I'm holding this phone?"

Nakamura tried calling back, but the phone suddenly went dead.

Nakamura had been a food detective long enough to know when something smelled fishy. Nakamura watched as the van was loaded on the back of a flatbed truck. "Stromboli, I'll meet you back at the station. I've got to make a little side trip." He walked over to his car and opened the door.

"Where are you heading?"

"Well, if I'm lucky, I'm going to say hello to the Nose, and maybe score a free lunch."

"And if you're unlucky?"

"Well, then I'm possibly heading into a dangerous situation. Keep your radio on."

"Well, I hope you get the lunch."

"Me too." Nakamura nodded, turned the ignition key, and sped off toward Chez Flambé.

Chapter Twenty-Three

On the Rack and on the Lamb

Neil ran as fast he could away from the library. If someone was after him, it wouldn't take them long to run back to the entrance and look around. He stuck to the alleyways. His nose and stomach urged him to stop at least twenty times. Neil could smell the most amazing cheeses, pâtés, and duck confit being served and prepared in hidden-away bistros. Neil knew the best, and best-priced, French food was available in these gems, far away from the eyes of the wealthier but food-ignorant tourists.

But Neil couldn't stop. He needed to find a safe place to stay, some new clothes, and then some food. His mind was racing as quickly as his heart and feet. The woman inside the *bibliothèque* had given him a lot to think about, and to be afraid of.

Part of him felt proud. The Flambés weren't just a bunch of overachieving capitalists, no matter what his parents had suggested. He was part of a long line of great chefs. He'd suspected this after reading the recipe book, but the woman had confirmed it.

On the flip side, he wasn't as super-special as he'd always thought. He wasn't The Great Flambé, he was A Great Flambé. And he wasn't even sure he was the best. This Flambé who was presumed killed had figured out the curse, and left clues hidden all over the place. He was a genius, and not just with food. What did Neil do? He got his restaurant decimated, then flew, alone and unarmed, halfway around the world despite being warned not to. Isabella was right. Sometimes he was too head-strong, too cocky.

Now he was in danger and out of contact with all his friends and family.

Neil stopped running and stood with his back against an alleyway wall. One more step and he'd be on a busy sidewalk. Hearing sirens in the distance he was reminded of the horrible image of a bloody Hugo Victoire pointing right at him, and suddenly his mind was racing. Was Hugo wounded, dead? Was he part of the order of the blue circle, or whatever they were

called? He'd shown Neil the 1291 date scratched into his door frame and had a spoon with the symbol. And why had Neil's silverware, with the same symbol, hurt the taste of his food?

The sirens grew louder. Were police looking for a redheaded boy who'd fled the scene? He spun around and spied a motorcycle turning down the far end of his alley. Was it a police officer? He couldn't risk it. He stepped into the crowd. The man on the motorcycle kept flying toward him.

Neil had to get away. He looked out across the street. There was a park there, with trees and bushes to hide behind. No Parisian would look twice at a tourist rushing through traffic, except to hope he got hit. Neil jumped into the street.

Cars flew right toward him. He ran so fast his hat flew off, clearly exposing his red hair. If anyone was looking for him, there were going to be plenty of witnesses. Neil stopped for a second to recover the hat but then saw a woman on a scooter heading right for him. She honked but showed no sign of slowing down. He turned and ran down the middle of the street between the still-moving cars. She honked again and stayed right on his tail. She seemed to be chasing him. Neil did his best to stay in front but in a matter of moments he was going to get run over.

Finally he spied a gap between two cars on his left and jumped through, landing in a heap on the sidewalk. The locals, cheered momentarily by the possibility of a dead tourist, glumly went back to haggling over baguettes and walking their tiny dogs.

The woman gave a final honk and continued on her way, weaving through the cars. The sirens continued to draw closer behind him.

Neil looked around for a way to escape. Just a few steps away he spied the entrance to a metro station. He made a dash for the stairs, knocking over a few angry locals on the way. A train was entering the station. He jumped the turnstile and ran past a sign that said METRO LINE 1. He smiled. This train ended in the last place anyone would look for him.

Neil had started his trip to Paris in the oldest part of the city, looking for the roots of the curse and the Flambé family tree. He'd found that. Now he needed to hide. He was going to head as far away from Vieux Paris as he could. He pulled his shirt collar as high as it would go and boarded the train. The doors closed, and Neil took a seat, waiting for the automated voice to call out La Defense.

La Defense bears no resemblance to the picture most people have in their heads when they hear the name Paris. There is no Eiffel Tower, no baroque opera house, no artsy cafés—just steel and glass office towers. Symbolically, the main road connecting the area to the rest of the city begins at the majestic Arc de Triomphe downtown, and ends in La Defense . . . with a giant, unadorned, shiny, ugly metal cube. La Defense was designed to be the economic hub of Paris, home to the business elite. A place for money and bankers to meet, not the pretty tree-lined streets of cafés and artists.

La Defense doesn't pretend to be pretty. It isn't.

Neil felt a sense of emptiness as he stepped out of the metro. There was no *here* here. No heart. A cool breeze ran down the man-made canyons, finding the seams in his clothing. *Good*, he thought. He felt confident that this was not the sort of place anyone would look for a French-food–loving chef.

"First things first; I need to do a little shopping." He walked into a nearby drugstore and gathered a few necessities, including a couple of new shirts. A few doors down Neil checked into a chain hotel, grabbing the smallest and cheapest room he could. He paid for everything in cash.

An hour later he was sitting on the end of his tiny bed with a towel wrapped around his head, kicking himself for not renting a room with a kitchenette. The room service menu resembled the weaker offerings at a burger joint. "We usually cater to American bankers and oil tycoons," the man at the front desk had said. "We could possibly run out and get you some Dijon mustard to go with your hamburger."

Neil had ended up ordering a house salad.

Neil carelessly picked at the limp greens and barely red tomatoes as he watched the local news describe the odd scene that morning outside Notre Dame Cathedral. Cameras captured the ambulances and police cars leaving the scene.

"The man, Hugo Victoire, is in Grace Hospital with life-threatening injuries. Police are searching for a young man with a large nose and red hair. He is possibly armed with a knife and is considered dangerous."

Neil walked into the bathroom and stared in the mirror. "There's nothing I can do about the nose," he said to himself. He unfurled the towel, revealing the result of his homemade dye job. "But welcome to life as a blond."

Chapter Twenty-Four

Order Up

Neil didn't have the best sleep of his life. He was tired enough and the hotel—while not pretty—was quiet. The problem was that he had too much to think about. He'd stared at the ceiling for hours, projecting all the facts he had onto it like an imaginary bulletin board. Each fact fit in its own illustrated panel, just like the book he'd read at the library, and together they would tell a story, if he could just put them in the right order.

He moved them around in his mind. In 1291 his ancestor had ticked off some sadistic group of knights by helping the people they were trying to kill. Pierre had been a member of the order himself, but betrayed them. Neil had seen the images. Many of those people Pierre saved had been young children and families, and they were starving to death.

Neil wondered what he would have done. It seemed odd for a Flambé to help someone else. It didn't come naturally to them. Of course, Neil did give Margarita money to help rebuild her kitchen in Mexico City. Isabella and Angel were always pushing him to do more charity work. It had made him feel better inside, about himself and, oddly, the world, but was it something he planned on making a regular habit? Probably not.

Besides, was that one act of betrayal really worth a thousand years of being cursed? And did Neil even believe in curses? He certainly didn't believe in magic. He'd assumed there was a logical answer behind all his bad luck. That's why he'd been so certain Stanley Picón and Deep Blue Cheese were the masterminds behind this whole business. It had made sense, but Larry had been right. There were too many unanswered threads, even before Picón told Neil he was "just a subcontractor."

Neil had used the phone in his room to call Larry and Isabella, but was forced to leave messages. Then he'd noticed the fee for even dialing an outside line was ten euros, so he decided to stop. There wasn't much anyone could do with him over here in France.

He'd come to Paris alone. That had been dumb. He'd gotten some answers. Maybe he needed to head back home and get back to work. Larry must have cleaned up the restaurant by now. He was allowed to open again. Maybe a big reopening party . . .

That was when he'd finally fallen asleep.

Now awake, blond, and hungry, he needed to make a decision. Home was looking like the best option. He needed to forget this wild goose chase and get back to work. Whoever was behind the curse had already known where to find him. Why sit around Paris when he could wait in Vancouver? Could he fly back unnoticed? His stomach growled again. He needed to eat before deciding on his next step.

Neil looked at the room service menu for breakfast. "Eggs and bacon with Texas toast and American-style coffee? I think the actual plastic menu has a better chance of being edible." A thought occurred to him. What would Larry do? Larry had a knack for finding the perfect joints for morning pick-me-ups. "I've got the same hair color as Larry now; maybe I'll find it easier to act like him." He decided to go for a walk to clear his mind and fill his stomach.

As he'd hoped, everyone in La Defense was too wrapped up in their cell phones and stock market quotes to notice some blond kid in a sweater vest and jeans. That was good, because Neil spent a long time wandering the streets. Even a hungry Neil Flambé was a discerning chef, and the first thirty or so shops he passed offered instant coffee and—the anathema of a real chef—croissants that had been premade, frozen, thawed, and then baked.

Neil wanted to cry.

Then a breeze came up and he caught a whiff of fresh

pastry. He sniffed. It was amazing, nearly perfect, and it was coming from a block or so away. He scanned the horizon. It was all steel and concrete. Was his nose playing tricks? Neil walked over slowly, sniffing the air like a bloodhound on a trail, looking for a tucked-away patisserie or café. Instead, he found himself standing in front of the blandest office tower he'd ever seen. He looked up, up, and up. There were no signs, no balconies, no decorative carvings . . . nothing except concrete and glass. It looked a giant fortress.

Yuck. You have to be really rich to build something that ugly, Neil thought. *And really desperate to look for quality food inside.*

Neil started to walk away, when a courier walked through the revolving doors and a fresh wave of baked awesome hit him. It wasn't Hugo's croissants, but it smelled almost as good. His stomach growled and his nose twitched. His body certainly wanted him to go through that door to find the source of this scent. "Well, into the breach, I guess." Neil followed his nose and went through the doors and into the lobby.

The lobby wasn't any more interesting than the exterior. The walls and the floor were all constructed from slick black stone and steel. The ceiling was barely a foot above Neil's head. The room seemed to suck up the light, and Neil had to concentrate to determine where the walls ended and the ceiling began.

"I've seen prisons with more charm." Neil whispered this, but the sound echoed off the walls and sent it back to him like a yell. *Creepy.* He didn't say this out loud. He turned to leave, but out of the corner of his eye he saw a flash of light. He walked over and saw that there was one tiny square of glass in the wall to his left. It turned out to be the window of a door, almost hidden in the flatness of the wall. The smell of the baking was seeping through the thin opening near the hinges. Neil opened the door and the aroma rushed over him, nearly overloading his senses. He opened his eyes and then had to rub them in disbelief. The door didn't open into another bland, featureless room, but into a classic, almost perfect, patisserie.

A woman was working behind the counter with her back to Neil, stacking racks of freshly made croissants, macaroons, tarts, baguettes, and small candied cakes that looked like miniature works of art.

"*Excusez-moi, madame.* Can I have a croissant, *s'il vous plait.*"

She didn't turn around but motioned with her thumb for Neil to take a seat. Even the service was classically French. It was like he'd stepped through a magic door that transported him from La Defense to the magical cafés of Montparnasse. The only difference was that this patisserie had no windows looking out to the street. It seemed to be completely contained within the lobby.

Neil turned back to the counter but the woman had gone. Neil grabbed a copy of *Le Monde* from the front table and sat down. He seemed to be the only one here. He checked his watch. It was 10:30, between the morning rush and the pre-lunch coffee break. He opened the paper. There was a picture of Hugo on page three. The accompanying story said police were asking for the public's help in locating a red-headed teenager.

A very thin and pale waiter scurried over and silently

laid a coffee and a fresh croissant in front of Neil. Neil tried to wave the coffee away, but the man insisted. "Eet, uh, comes weeth le croissant. Eet eez very good."

"Um, *merci*," Neil said. The waiter started to walk away, but Neil touched his arm and looked up at him.

"If you don't mind my asking, why is this place here?"

"Ow do you uh, mean, monsieur?"

"Well, it's not on the street or near a window, it's right in the middle of an ugly building and yet I can tell the food is wonderful. And it looks like a classic café or patisserie."

"Ah, zee café waz here long before zee buildings were constructed. It eez very old, I think. When they decide to, uh, beeld zis building, zey keep zis place in its, uh . . . place."

"Hmmm. Interesting. *Merci*," Neil said again.

The waiter nodded and left the bill under the coffee cup.

Neil sniffed the croissant. It was certainly not some prefab doughy disaster. He took a bite, and it flaked beautifully, like crispy whipped butter. His stomach, nose, and tongue all applauded. He smiled, and savored the next three bites as much as the first.

Then he looked at the steaming cup of coffee. What was it Larry found so great about this stuff? Neil always liked the smell, and he frequently used coffee in some of his pastries and even as part of the coating for some of his meat dishes. But every time he tasted coffee on his own, he felt like he was licking the bottom of an ashtray. Maybe he was drinking the wrong coffee? The croissant had been exquisite, perhaps the coffee was better here as well.

He raised the cup to his nose. It smelled very good, rich, almost chocolaty. He lifted it to his lips and took a sip. It wasn't too bitter, maybe a swallow? "Bleecch," he said as the warm liquid went over his taste buds and down his throat. He put the cup back down quickly and struck out his tongue. He needed another croissant—or three—to get rid of that taste.

Instantly a plate appeared in front of him. It wasn't a croissant this time but a sticky raisin bun.

"Um, no thanks, *non merci*, waiter. I'd actually like to order another couple of croissants, *s'il vous plaît*." The plate disappeared and then reappeared with another sticky bun—but this time with a white frosted cross built into the pastry.

"Um. No, thank you." Neil felt a chill run down his spine, but he fought to stay cool. Maybe it was an odd coincidence, or maybe he needed to leave and fast. "I need to be going." He reached for the bill and noticed three things at once. The hand that was offering him the crossed-bun didn't belong to the waiter, the knife on the plate next to the bun was stamped with a circle and cross, and the address on the bill was "1291 rue le jour."

Then everything went black and Neil's head fell to the table. Only the sugary bun cushioned the blow.

Chapter Twenty-Five

Messy Situations

Nakamura parked his car outside Chez Flambé. Nakamura was hoping Larry might be hanging around the place. He wanted to ask Larry about renting the van. The rental agency had written the number of the driver's license down and it matched Larry's. A photocopy would have been better, so they could see if the license had been altered at all, or if Larry had really rented the van himself.

Nakamura had seen enough fraud cases, and minors faking ID, to know a driver's license was no guarantee of a person's identity.

But it wasn't Larry whom he saw through the window of the restaurant, it was the Soba twins. They were busily sweeping up the rubble, and had even separated the fridge door from the wall.

Nakamura knocked at the front door. Amber walked over

with a big smile. "Hey, Sean, what brings you here? Party's not until tomorrow!"

"So you do know about the party?"

"Yeah, of course. Neil texted us a couple of hours ago and asked us to get the place cleaned up. At this rate we'll be here right up until the party starts!"

Zoe called over from a pile of broken table legs she'd stacked up. "Destruction's more our thing, but there's some great debris here we can use for a new sculpture we're working on. And this is some killer overtime!"

Nakamura held up his gold envelope. "Did you make the invitations?"

Amber took it from him and looked it over. "It's pretty good, but it's not our work. The gold paper's not really our style."

"Gold paper?" Zoe said, walking over and looking at the invitation. "Hey, I recognize this stuff."

"It's special somehow?" Nakamura asked.

"It's edible."

"Edible?"

"Yeah, the paper isn't really paper. It's made from rice. The gold is edible too, and it's woven in. Neil used to bring it out for special desserts."

"He'd serve, like, chocolate wafers and stuff inside an envelope made from the paper. The customers would open it like a letter and then eat the whole thing."

"Larry called them Neil's memo-munchies."

Zoe nodded. "Neil had a whole stack of this stuff. I think he actually kept it in his safe. It's pretty expensive."

"In the safe?"

Amber nodded.

"The same safe that was stolen last week?" Nakamura pulled out his notebook and started comparing dates. "The safe was stolen before the health department closed down the restaurant for a week. So how could Neil throw a reopening party, with printed invitations, before he knew the restaurant was going to be closed?"

Amber and Zoe shrugged. "Dunno. Maybe he's psychic. He's been acting really strange lately."

Zoe nodded. "Stranger than usual."

"This isn't adding up." Nakamura said. He walked over to the notice Greta Carbo had put up on the window. It had been torn in half by the force of the blast. Nakamura looked around the floor but couldn't find the bit with the health department number on it. "Either of you see a strip of red paper with a phone number on it?"

Zoe pointed at the pile of rubble she was sweeping into a pail. "Is that a serious question?"

"Never mind. I'll call Stromboli." Nakamura dialed his partner.

"Stromboli here. How's the free lunch?"

"Tastes like plaster dust. Look, Stromboli, I need you to get ahold of Greta Carbo in the health department. I think she needs to come over and check out Chez Flambé. And I need to ask her a few questions."

"You got it. I'll call you back."

Nakamura clicked his phone shut. He looked at the health notice again, and then something caught his eye out on the street. The road crew seemed to have finally finished paving the road. That was a good sign. But something was glowing in the window of the pet shop/restaurant across the street. The two blue dots were still visible through the grime. Something had triggered the motion sensor. Had the rats returned?

"I'll be right back," he said to the twins. He walked over to the still-vacant storefront and tried the handle. It was locked. He peered through the grime as best he could. He couldn't make out anything moving, but the blue dots looked different, almost like they were flickering.

He walked over to the big front window. It was even grimier than the door. The lights did indeed seem to be flickering, like candles. Sean noticed something else as he stared at the construction permit in the window. It had also been signed by Greta Carbo. Odd. There was a phone number underneath her name. Nakamura dialed it.

"You have reached the voice mail of Greta Carbo at Vancouver Public Works. Please leave a message after the beep." Nakamura was about leave a message when his phone began to vibrate, signaling another call.

He clicked answer.

"Stromboli here, Inspector. I called the Health Department. This is weird. . . ."

"What?"

"They say there's no one there named Greta Carbo."

Chapter Twenty-Six

Siege the Day

Neil's head throbbed. It also smelled like icing sugar. The memory flooded back. "Ohhh, I am such an idiot," he moaned. He half hoped Larry would come up with some kind of witty putdown, but Larry wasn't here. Neil was alone, in a pitch-dark room. "Why did I drink that coffee? Coffee sucks!" he yelled. His amplified words echoed back to him.

His stomach rumbled again. He reached up to wipe the frosting off his head and was a bit surprised to find that he could. His hands weren't tied or handcuffed. He greedily licked his fingers. The sugar seemed to take the edge off his headache, and he stood up. So his feet weren't tied either. He slowly walked around the room, feeling the walls to make sure he wasn't going to fall down any hidden stairs. He was in a cube of some sort. He tapped the walls. Stone. He couldn't even feel any seams where doors or windows should be.

His stomach rumbled again and he felt dizzy. He slid back down a wall and sat on the floor.

Then he heard a loud crack, followed by footsteps— someone in heavy boots by the sound of it. Where the heck were those coming from? A light suddenly shone down on his head and he had to close his eyes. The light was so intense his head began to throb again.

"Ah, the traitor is awake." It was a woman's voice, but not one Neil recognized. He could detect a slight accent but he couldn't place it.

"Where am I? Who the heck are you?" Neil said, shielding his eyes.

"I am many people." Her voice lowered and she spoke with a German accent, all the time walking toward Neil. "I am a German businessman who buys decrepit pet shops."

"Carrion," Neil said, gritting his teeth.

"I am a crazy Vespa driver on the streets of Paris. *Bougez-vous, idiot!*" she yelled, and Neil recognized the helmeted woman who had chased him into the metro.

"And I am also a very good actor." Her voice lowered again and she sounded just like a man. "Perhaps you saw me in that great film about the thrilling kidnapping of the King of France!"

Neil remembered the actors he'd seen chatting at the Lunchback Café. One had been a woman? "Nice beard," he said. "Was that real or fake?"

"It's a shame I had to deal with Hugo like that. But he told you so much, before I was ready. You see, more than anything, I am the sworn enemy of anyone cursed enough to be born a Flambé and stupid enough to become a chef." It was the woman's voice again, this time right next to his face.

Neil's eyes began to adjust to the light. He blinked as the woman's face slowly began to come into focus.

"Greta Carbo," Neil said. "So you do talk. But I presume that's not your real name either, is it?"

"*Mais non,*" she said, standing up. "My real name is Jeanne Valette."

"Valette. Of course it is. And you're here to put a curse on me and my family," Neil scowled. He'd walked right into a trap—something he'd done regularly for about a year—but this time he had no plan for how to escape.

"That curse was laid centuries ago, by my great ancestor, after that pitiful Pierre Flambé betrayed him and the rest of the world."

"From what I've heard Valette was a bit of a jerk. Runs in the family, clearly."

She leaned down and slapped Neil's face lightly, pouting her lips. "You Flambés are such pains. So stupid, so cocky. I can't wait to see you suffer."

"This isn't suffering? Your breath stinks."

She slapped him, harder this time, and stood up. "You Flambés make me sick."

Neil tried to stand up as well but his legs felt weak and he slumped back down to the floor. "You drugged me," he said.

"Yes. How did you like the sedative in the coffee?"

"It was bitter, like you."

"Such a brave, stupid little boy. I was hoping for a

much tougher time destroying you. You see, there's a pattern your ancestors followed. Teenage prodigies, then adult tragedies. You are already a tragedy and you're barely more than a child. Sad. You naive Flambés have always been so easy to defeat."

"Defeat? I took your little computer buddy for a cool hundred thousand bucks."

Valette actually doubled over with laughter. "A hundred thousand dollars? Seriously? That piece of marble you're resting your pathetic little butt on costs more than that. And thanks to Picón's little exploding tuna can there's at least that much in damage at Chez . . . Chez Flatulence, is it?"

Neil growled.

Valette continued. "I told Picón that explosion would be redundant, given what I have planned, but he insisted."

"What do you mean 'what I have planned'?"

"All in good time. That reminds me . . ."

Valette pulled a cellphone out of her pocket and flipped it open. Neil realized with a jolt that it was his. She began texting something, then hit send and smiled, clicking the phone shut.

"What did you just do?" Neil said, gritting his teeth.

"I'm just making sure my plan is still moving ahead. You just sent another little reminder out to all your friends."

"Reminder of what? Isn't taking me prisoner the plan? I can't cook if you keep me here. That's the curse isn't it, not cooking ever again? Or maybe this is some kind of silly siege? Maybe you're going to starve me like your ancestor wanted to starve those people in the town? Maybe you're going to keep me here as a prisoner like those other knights were kept prisoner . . . ?"

"Tsk, tsk. You really don't understand revenge, do you?" she said, with a kind of mock-motherly gaze. "Let me explain it in a way that your puny little brain can understand."

"Don't bother. I know what happened in 1291. I know that Flambés throughout history have had their careers, their lives, destroyed by you and your family. This curse needs to end. It's crazy to hold me responsible for something that happened a thousand years ago. You just said you're rich, why bother keeping this up?"

Valette frowned. "Do you see this?" She raised her sleeve, revealing her arm and a dark blue tattoo of the circle and cross. "This is the symbol of our order. We were chefs to knights, kings, Popes. We were on the verge of taking back the Holy Land. Those 'innocent' families that idiot Flambé wanted to help were the remnants of the best soldiers of the infidel's army. That act of betrayal didn't just cost us the battle, or Valette and the others a few years of freedom. It cost us the WORLD." She clenched her fists and took a deep angry breath. "The world," she hissed.

"It was a thousand years ago. It's ancient history," Neil said.

"The fight is still going on, you idiot, or maybe you don't read the newspapers. There are still wars, battles.

We could have cleaned them off the face of the earth; we were this close." She leaned down and pinched her fingers together around Neil's nose. A shot of pain gripped Neil's skull. He held his head in his hands, rocking, waiting for the pain to ebb.

She grabbed his chin and looked into his eyes. "I like you, Flambé, I really do. There's a cruelty in your eyes. Part of me would like to see you keep fighting other chefs, mocking them, flaunting your superior skills, destroying them. I almost don't want to ruin you. You could be great. But then you go and do silly things, like give money to feed Mexican orphans, or give that idiot cousin of yours a job when he should probably be in jail or begging for nickels on the street. That's weakness, and that can't be allowed. So the part of me that doesn't want to destroy you is easily ignored."

"I'm guessing you blame weakness for what Pierre Flambé did to save those people. They were starving."

"Lies. Believing them just shows how weak you Flambés still are. I am the president and CEO of this company. We run a global empire making and selling almost anything you can imagine—food, weapons, movies . . ."

"Murder . . . ," Neil said through gritted teeth.

"Do you think this fortune was built on helping the weak? Or on crushing them?" As if in answer, she gripped Neil's arm until he cried out in pain.

She let go. "You see . . . weak. The people around you have helped make you weak, of course. That Angel Jícama, with his 'simplify and be happy' garbage. Isabella Tortellini with her organic flower water. What a pathetic collection of fools. Thank goodness they won't be around to keep giving you such silly advice much longer."

Neil felt his chest heave with a sense of dread. "What . . . What are you going to do? Don't you dare hurt anyone else!"

"It's too late. You see, I bought that dump across from you—"

"—to start a rival restaurant. Carrion. I guessed that already."

Valette scoffed. "Only an idiot would try to run a restaurant in that slum. Carrion was there for two reasons. One, it was like an itch that you kept wanting to scratch for days and days. 'Who's there? What is that place? Who's out to get me?' It's amazing what kind of torture you can put yourself through with a little prodding and your own paranoia. I learned that in the army."

"That where you met Picón?"

"Yes." She lowered her voice again and spoke with a Southern accent. "Don't you remember meeting a Southern Colonel, kid?"

"Have you been backing all my enemies?"

"Some. You've done a good job of making plenty on your own. Of course, I've helped push here and there. It was pretty easy to get Carlotta Calamari interested in Marco Polo's journey, and help pay some of her travel costs. I've been a patron to all of Giselle Calabaza's trips. Picón is a protégé, of course, as well as a few chefs you haven't met . . . yet."

"So all these people have been part of the plan against me for years?"

"I don't let anyone else in on the plans. Loose lips

sink ships, you know. I just back them in their personal
endeavors to destroy you. You've heard of venture capitalists? I'm a sort of vendetta capitalist. Once you turned
fifteen, it was apparent they couldn't do it on their own.
It was time for me to be personally involved."

Neil felt as if the whole world were crashing down around him. He knew this was exactly what Valette wanted him to feel, so he fought against it, but it was a struggle. "You said Carrion was there for two reasons?"

"Ah, yes. Reason number two. You have invited all the people you love to a grand reopening party at Chez Flambé. Your parents are coming, and even that idiot on the police force, Nakamura. Oh, and you made sure to invite all your suppliers as well." She held up a red binder that Neil recognized as his personal address book.

"You stole the safe?"

"Your friend Berger did that for me. He's not very bright, either. Same modus operandi as last time. Just leave him an envelope with some money and Cheez Doodles—and incredibly simple instructions—and he'll do anything, especially if it will hurt you."

"You're insane and you're rambling."

"I'm in no hurry." She shrugged. "I'm just waiting until I turn on the TV screen that's hidden in the wall over there and show you the funeral you've organized."

"I thought you said it was a party!"

"Oh, it is a party and it's going to be a blast." She began to chuckle. "Oh my, it's such a shame that that road crew weakened the sewer underneath the road. The gas lines run right next to the sewer, you know. And just as everyone arrives for the party, the road is going to sink in, severing all the gas lines and turning the entire block into a fireball."

"That's where the rats came from! You've been digging underneath the road!"

"Ah, you're not as dumb as you look. I'm afraid the

workers who did that job for me are still down there. They really should have checked to make the sure the mushrooms in the risotto I sent them were really portobello. And they really shouldn't smoke down there. Of course the great thing about a really good gas explosion is that it destroys everything, including all the evidence."

Neil's phone began to beep.

"Not *all* the evidence. There's plenty that will be pointing at you, including Hugo's corpse, the calls from your phone. And the alarm clock on your phone that is set for a specific time—kind of like a remote detonator. Now. Time to stop talking and start watching. The camera inside Carrion should capture the whole scene." Valette pulled a remote out of her tiny pocket and clicked a button. One of the stones in the far wall slid back and away. A TV screen began to slide forward, humming to life.

She let the hand with Neil's phone fall to her side.

Neil summoned up all his strength and anger and made a lunge for the phone. He stretched out, just grabbing the phone as he knocked into the back of Valette's legs. She slid away from him on the slick floor, slamming into the wall under the TV.

Neil grabbed his phone. The sent text message was still on the screen. "See you soon, Neil." He fumbled to unlock the keyboard. Like Larry, Neil had bought a new phone after the Azteca Cocina, but unlike Larry he hadn't figured out all the functions.

Valette stood up, and calmly smoothed her outfit. "You can call, but it's too late. Your beloved dump will soon take the lives of everyone you hold dear."

"Kill me instead!" Neil yelled, trying to remember if he was supposed to press # or *. Valette had done so many things to rattle his brain, his confidence, and now, when he needed them most, he was failing again.

She walked toward him and picked up the remote she'd dropped. "Kill you? What kind of revenge is that? Just think of what the rest of your life is going to be like. You rose so far so fast, and that's when I noticed you. Like your great-grandfather, who made rations for the army and made sure his name was stamped on them. What an egotistical jerk. That's how we knew the Flambés were still alive and in the United States. He'd already had kids by then, but they couldn't cook. You, with your duels and interviews and TV appearances, were easier to find."

"Don't hurt them."

"*You're* about to, and you will suffer forever. You won't even want to cook again. That's the real curse. You bring about your own destruction. You bring the world nothing but misery and death and that's all the Flambés have EVER DONE!"

Her face contorted in a cruel grin as she pointed the remote over her shoulder at the TV. "You'll always know that you did THIS." The TV flicked on just as Neil pressed * and dialed Larry.

The TV showed a completely empty Chez Flambé, with a smiling Sean Nakamura in front, along with a crew of workers from the Terine Gas Company. The restaurant wasn't destroyed!

Neil shook with relief. Tears welled in his eyes. He

smiled. Valette saw the look in Neil's eyes and swung around with an angry scream. "NOOOOOO!" Nakamura walked up to the window of Carrion and waved for the camera.

Just then Neil's phone vibrated and a message flashed up on the phone's screen.

DUCK

Chapter Twenty-Seven

Duck, Duck, Duck . . . Goosed

At any other time, Neil would have assumed this was an advance order for one of his amazing dishes. Now, in his current situation, he knew it was a warning.

He threw himself flat on the floor just as a huge panel from the wall behind him flew through the air and smashed into the TV. Valette turned around with a crazed expression and clicked another button on the remote.

Immediately dozens of small gas canisters fell down from the ceiling. In a split second the room was filled with smoke. Someone ran up to Neil and slipped a mask over his face. Neil looked up to see who it was, but the smoke obscured everything above the knees. Then he recognized the shoes. He'd seen them just the day before outside his bathroom stall.

Jean-Claude Chili. The shoes raced off in the direction of Valette. Neil could see her shoes as well, running away in the far distance, then the gas settled to the floor and everything was lost in a wash of gray.

Neil stood up, still feeling wobbly. Chili needed help. Neil wasn't sure he could be much help, but he had to try. He took a step, but his legs felt like rubber. With no way to tell where he was, he lost his balance and fell backward.

"Whoa there, captain," said a muffled voice. "Never try to moonwalk when you've been drugged."

"Larry!" was all Neil could say.

The gas started to dissipate and Larry spied Neil's hair.

"Hey! A little more platinum than mine, but I'm flattered you want to be more like me."

Neil couldn't say anything. He just hugged his cousin. Finally he spurted out, "I'm . . . sorry. I was such an idiot coming here alone."

"You still would have been an idiot if you'd brought someone else along. Kind of a dumb plan from the start, really."

"How did you find me?"

"I'll explain later. We've got some work to do. Hold on to my arm. We've got to get to the stairs. Jones should be around here somewhere." They shuffled back toward the hole that had been blasted in the wall.

"Jones?"

"Yeah, you should have seen him on the flight over. He was like a kid going to the circus. I think he's been itching for a fight. Isabella is downstairs somewhere, keeping an eye on the security guards. She made sure they didn't tip off Valette. Of course that would have been hard to do since they were all knocked unconscious by Jones."

"He used gas?"

"Um, this is Jones we're talking about."

"He used his hands?"

"Let's just say that I highly recommend staying on Isabella's good side."

They reached the hole and Larry began grabbing more of the stone panels, ripping them loose to widen the opening. The wall fell apart more easily than Neil expected, opening up a virtual doorway.

"Been working out?" Neil asked.

"Nope. Great thing about cracking a fortress wall, once you make even a small hole the entire structure is weakened."

"Let me guess. You've been discussing siege tactics with Adrianne Tortosa."

"Yup, gave her a call just before I caught the plane. I promised I'd bring back some book she wanted from an antique dealer over on the left bank."

Larry helped Neil avoid the rubble on the ground as they shuffled toward the stairs. The air was clearing and Larry slipped his mask onto the top of his head and took

a deep breath. "That's better. Those things are stuffy."

Neil could see the bags around Larry's eyes. He clearly hadn't slept well lately. Neil felt a lump in his throat and his eyes watered. He took off his mask and wiped his eyes with his sleeve.

"Think you can make it down a few flights of stairs?" Larry said. "Or should we rest?"

"I'm feeling better," Neil said. They pushed open the door and started to walk down the first steps. Neil used the railing and Larry for support.

"We're on the top floor, so actually it's more like sixty flights of stairs. Let's go!"

"You're kidding," Neil said, groaning.

"Yeah. It's actually seventy. But I want to keep your hopes up. Hey, I think I see Jones down there!"

Neil leaned over the railing. Jones was down about ten stories, waving his arms at Neil and Larry. He seemed to be yelling something but a loud whooshing noise drowned out the words.

"He's saying hi. HI, JONES!" Larry yelled, waving back. Jones stopped waving and started shaking his fist. Then he pointed toward the ground floor and waved his arms again.

"He's telling us to get out of here," Neil said. "I think we'd better listen." Just then Jones jumped out of sight as the source of the whooshing noise became apparent; a giant fireball was flying up the stairwell. Neil could make out the smell of singed baked goods in the warm wind that hit his face. "It's the gas ovens from that café. They've exploded. It must have been built right below the stairwell."

Larry tried the door. It was locked. "Um, I think maybe we should go back up the stairs, and fast," Larry said in a shaky voice. He grabbed Neil's arms and they rushed up two steps at a time. Neil, still fighting against the effects of the drugged coffee, fell. The air grew hotter by the second. Neil pointed up the stairwell past Larry.

"If you say 'go on without me,' I'll puke," Larry said, bending down to help Neil stand.

"I'm not a suicidal moron, you idiot. You said we were on the top floor. I was pointing to that hatch on the ceiling. I think it opens onto the roof."

Larry looked up. There was a small attic ladder bolted flat against the ceiling. The rope to pull it down had been cut or was missing.

"Now lift me up!"

There was no time to lose. In one motion Larry lifted Neil up and onto his shoulders. Neil reached out and grabbed the bottom rung. It slid down on its hinges like an accordion. The whoosh was almost deafening now.

Neil ran up the ladder, Larry just behind him. Neil shoved against the hatch door, which opened with a groan. Together he and Larry flung themselves into the roof just as a plume of flame and smoke shot up out of the opening.

Neil lay on the hot tar-and-gravel roof, breathing hard. "I hope Jones was smart enough to prop his door open when he went into the stairwell to warn us about the booby trap."

"I wouldn't worry. He's strong enough to yank it open. I'm more worried about what that hatch door is going to do if it blows off." The hatch was hanging by a single hinge and was twisting ominously in the fire and smoke.

"We'd better look for some safe cover," Larry said. They looked around. The roof was covered with numerous satellite dishes, hulking metal transformer boxes, and air conditioners. All were marked with DANGER ELECTRICAL stickers, and painted with the blue cross and circle. "Is there anything Valette Incorporated *doesn't* manufacture?" Larry said.

Suddenly a gunshot rang out, scattering the stones at Larry's feet. He jumped in the air. "Yikes! That was close." Neil got to his feet as quickly as he could. Just a few feet away Chili and Valette were struggling over a gun. Chili had a cut above his right eye and his lip was bleeding. Valette's clothes were torn and a line of blood ran down the side of her head. She had a crazed expression on her face. She pulled the trigger, sending another bullet flying into the hulking transformer next to Neil's head.

Neil ducked behind it, then peeked around the side.

Chili had his hand on the gun barrel. Neil could see the pain in his eyes. That metal would be hot and the vibration surely shattered at least some of the bones in his hand. Yet he still held on. Neil wished he had something, a knife, a pot . . . anything.

Wait, he did have something.

Neil quickly grabbed the gas mask off his head and pulled the elastic back. It could work. If his ancient ancestor could use a slingshot catapult, then so could he. He grabbed a handful of the largest stones and put them in the mask.

"Good idea, cuz!" Larry said, jumping behind the

metal box and pulling off his own mask. They each grabbed a handful and then stepped out into the open. Chili looked like a boxer on the ropes, waiting for the inevitable knockout punch.

"Hey, nerdlinger! DUCK!" Larry yelled.

Chili dropped to the ground, smacking his head on Valette's boots, just as Larry and Neil let the stones fly. The stones pelted Valette in the body and face. She screamed in pain and toppled toward the edge of the building. The gun flew from her hand and over the side. Chili didn't move.

She grabbed the railing and steadied herself, reeling from what felt like a hundred bee stings. "You . . . little . . . wretches. You won't beat me that easily." She stood up and smiled.

"What's she got to smile about?" Larry wondered, turning to Neil.

Suddenly, a loud whooshing noise rose up behind them and the wind became as strong as a hurricane. Neil looked back nervously, fearing another fireball. Instead he saw the rotors of a helicopter coming straight for his head, and Larry's.

"DUCK!" Neil yelled. He and Larry hit the gravel just in time as the helicopter buzzed right over them. It stopped to hover over Valette. Neil could see a giant blue circle and cross painted on the underbelly. The pilot was the waiter from Hugo's café.

"I see you have traitors instead of waiters!" Neil yelled.

"Your banter still needs work," Larry said and gave Neil a weak smile.

"*Au revoir!*" Valette yelled above the noise of the copter.

The pilot lowered a rope ladder down to Valette, who grabbed it and held tight. The copter rose and she was pulled into the air. She gave a wave and then pulled a cell phone from her pocket and dialed Neil's phone.

Neil answered. "We'll find you, you . . . jerk!" he spat.

"You won't even survive. The entire place is a booby trap," she said and smiled. "And I've set it to blow in five minutes. I said I didn't want to kill you, but you've left me little choice. It looks like you'll get your wish. The curse will end . . . with you. At least the Valettes can now continue the battle without any silly red-haired distractions." She hung up and the helicopter rose higher.

Neil grabbed his gas mask and attempted to shoot more stones up at the copter. "It's too far up there, cuz," Larry said. "Man, I wish I had a rocket launcher."

At that moment there was another explosion in the stairway behind them and the hatch shot into the air like a missile, slicing right through the motor of the helicopter.

"That'll work too." Larry smiled.

The copter lurched violently as the pilot attempted to keep it airborne. Valette gripped the ladder as it swung over the side of the building and back again. Smoke and flames poured from the motor. A loud mechanical whine filled the air as the rotors slowed. The copter swayed and then fell.

"Chili's right underneath!" Neil yelled. He and Larry ran over and grabbed Chili's unconscious body away from the falling wreck. They dragged him across the stones and behind a transformer. The copter gave one final lurch and then crashed right on the edge of the building. It teetered between falling down the side and falling back toward the roof. The copter tilted and the rotors smacked the metal and concrete. Bits of rotor flew in every direction. One flew right at Neil, Larry, and Chili, lodging itself in the metal transformer, which began to hiss and spit sparks and smoke.

"I think we'd better move," Larry said. They grabbed Chili and quickly headed toward one of the satellite dishes. As soon as they ducked down behind the concrete base, the dishes all started to rock and shift, as if they had suddenly come alive. "What the heck?" Larry said.

Another rotor flew into the roof behind them,

sending stones flying through the air like bullets, ripping holes in the other rooftop transformers, which also began to spit and smoke.

One last rotor clung loosely to the spinning metal hub. With a final revolution it cut into the body of the copter, shearing the cockpit in half. The pilot scrambled out just as the back fell down the side of the building. Neil looked up and saw the top of his head and his hands rising just above the roofline. He was clinging desperately to the top rung of the ladder. The rest of the smoldering hulk settled back onto the roof. The rope of the ladder began to unravel and the pilot's eyes grew wide with terror.

"We've got to go help him," Neil said.

He and Larry ran over, but before they could reach him the man's hands slipped and he disappeared. Neil and Larry stopped cold just a few feet from the edge.

"NO!" Neil shouted.

Then a hand rose over the edge of the building, reaching from rung to rung. Jeanne Valette's head appeared a moment later, as she pulled herself over the side and up the ladder. The rope unraveled more and she gritted her teeth. Neil took a step forward to help her. Larry grabbed his arm. "Careful. She's a loony."

The rope unraveled even more and Valette's head slipped below the roof edge.

"I can't just let her fall," Neil said. He jumped and grabbed the end of the rope ladder just as it snapped off the wreckage. The weight of Valette and the rope dragged him face-first toward the edge. He realized in a flash that if he didn't let go, he and the ladder were going to fly over the edge. "I'm sorry!" he yelled and began to loosen his grip. But just then Larry jumped in front of him and grabbed the rope, at the same time jamming his leg up against the railing. The ladder stopped falling.

"C'mon, Valette, get up here!" Larry yelled in pain as his knee twisted awkwardly. Neil held on and got to his feet, holding tight. He could feel the rope twitch as Valette made her way back up to the roof. She climbed over the edge and collapsed on the stones.

Larry and Neil pulled up the ladder. Valette had been the only person holding on.

Neil walked over to her. "I'm sorry we couldn't save the pilot. He fell. You're lucky he didn't hit you on the way down."

Valette got to her feet and grinned. "He didn't fall. I threw him down."

"What?" Neil said, shocked.

Valette calmly brushed the dirt off her clothes. "He was in my way. Besides, if he kept holding on to the ladder, we'd both have fallen to our deaths. It's like I said to you before, the Valettes have risen to the top by getting rid of the weak, not helping them."

Larry shook his head. "You are a piece of work, you know that? Well, I guess the only good news is that we all die together now, including you. Unless you turn off the self-destruct sequence."

"Oh, I don't think so." She sneered. "I mean, yes, you'll be dead soon. But like the master of any good fortress, I've got my own backup plan." She walked over to the wreckage of the copter and stepped inside.

"What are you going to do, fly it?" Larry called over.

Valette stepped back onto the roof, with a parachute strapped to her shoulders. "There are two. I've got one. Now we'll see how weak you really are. Which one gets the second chute? Which one of you lives?"

She threw the chute at Neil's feet and then walked to the edge of the roof and climbed up on the railing.

Isabella jumped in her chair as a giant explosion shook the building. She ran over and stuck her head outside the door of the security room. The odd café in the lobby was on fire. The walls were intact but the tempered glass window in the door was glowing with a intense white flame. Isabella had seen the inside of the ovens where her glass perfume bottles were made. This looked like that. But the door seemed to be holding fast.

She looked at the security guards Jones had tied up in the middle of the security room floor. The blast hadn't shaken them awake, thank goodness. She was pretty sure there was no way any of them could do anything even if they were awake, but Isabella didn't want that theory tested.

Isabella walked back to the bank of television screens on the wall. Screen after screen began to go dark as the security cameras in the stairwell began to burn. There were seventy in all, one for each floor. She looked ahead to the last screen and gasped.

She could make out two figures trying to reach for something in the ceiling. The heat from the flames distorted the image, like the sun on a steaming-hot highway, but could it be Neil and Larry? Screen after screen, racing toward the final image. Isabella watched helplessly as the two figures hammered and banged on the ceiling.

There was a glimmer of light from above them, and then that screen went dark as well. She hoped the glimmer was proof that the two had gotten out in time. There was no way to find out. The roof seemed to be camera-free. She had to believe they were safe.

Isabella fell back into her chair, feeling useless. Neil and Larry were on the roof. Jones and that strange man named Chili were also in the building somewhere, likely in danger, and she was watching over a bunch of knocked-out security guards.

"There has to be something I can do while I'm waiting," she said to the unconscious group on the floor. She stared at the giant console that lined the wall under the TV screens. Hundreds of glowing buttons and switches stared back. "There are way too many buttons for a simple surveillance room. Maybe one of these buttons turns off the flames, or maybe turns on a sprinkler system . . . or the roof cameras." She walked up and down the console, examining the buttons.

One was clearly labeled with an image of a fire. She flicked the switch. Immediately she could hear a loud hiss as high-powered sprinklers in the café began to douse the flames.

"So far so good," she said.

"Now, what about this one?" She pushed a button

with a symbol of a satellite. The few TV screens that were tuned to regular TV shows began to show electronic snow. "That's not very useful," she said.

She pushed another button, but the TVs still oscillated between snow and clear image. She tried a number of switches and buttons in combination.

All of a sudden the lights went off and a large red

lamp rose from the top of the console and began to spin around, casting the entire room in an eerie red glow. "*Cosa?* What did I do?" she said. She pushed a few more buttons and flicked a few more switches.

A digital clock rose from out of the wall, with a countdown.

5:00, 4:59, 4:58. 4:57 . . .

Five minutes until what? What had she done?

The door to the room burst open.

"Isabella, here, now!" Jones yelled. Isabella stared at the clock. It continued to count down.

She ran over. Jones's suit was scorched, and he smelled like smoke. Together they bolted for the front door.

Just as they were about to go through, a giant smoldering chunk of metal crashed in front of the door. Bits of metal and glass flew at them, cracking the tempered glass and bending the metal. Flames poured from the wrecked copter. Jones struggled against the revolving door, but it was now jammed shut. The bulk of the cockpit came to rest in front of the emergency exit. There was no leaving this way.

"There has to be a back door," Isabella said.

Jones shook his head. "I looked when we first came in, planning whatever escape we might need. This place is built like a castle, literally. One way in, one way out . . . and that way is now blocked."

Isabella knew the clock continued to count down, and she had a pretty good idea that when it hit zero, bad things were going to happen. "Follow me," she said. They ran back into the security room.

2:53, 2:52, 2:51 . . .

"Look for anything that seems like a cancel button," she said.

"I've got a better idea." Jones walked over and knelt down next to the guards. He examined their badges and picked the one with the highest rank. Then he reached into his own back pocket and pulled out a small paper container. He held it under the man's nose and cracked it open. The man immediately took a sharp breath and woke up.

"All right, listen to me and listen good," Jones said, grabbing the man by the shoulders and shaking him. "We've got two minutes until we all die, unless you tell me how to stop that clock."

The man shook his head, which began to bob down to his chest again. Jones slapped him across the cheek. "Wake up and focus! WE . . . ARE . . . GOING . . . TO . . . DIE . . ."

The man's head bobbed down again.

Jones slapped him again, but the man shook his head. He was awake. Jones could see it in his eyes. His jaw must hurt too much to speak. Jones had probably cracked it, a decision he was beginning to regret.

The man bobbed his head down again.

"He's pointing at his chest," Isabella said.

Jones pointed at the man's shirt pocket. "Here?" The man shook his head.

"It's inside his shirt," Isabella yelled. "He must have a key or something." She searched the entire console for any sign of a special lock. Jones tore the man's shirt off.

He had a set of keys on a chain around his neck. "Great, it couldn't be a simple one-key or a pass card."

1:30, 1:29, 1:28 . . .

He ripped the keys off the man's chest and threw them to Isabella.

"Where is the lock?" she yelled. "Untie him!"

"I can't. There's no time." Jones didn't tie up prisoners with any knot that could be undone quickly, and he'd used wire this time, not rope. He hadn't wanted to leave Isabella in any danger. He was kicking himself now. He couldn't even lift the guy, there were five guards tied together.

Jones stared into the man's eyes. "Where is the keypad?"

The man stared at Isabella. She began to point at different spot on the console. He shook his head. She continued down the length of the console, pointing. Finally, at the very end the man began to vigorously nod.

"There's nothing here," she said.

Jones ran over and stared at the flat metal. He slammed his fist on the console, denting the surface. A gap appeared where the top of a panel was hidden. He shoved his fingers underneath and lifted, ripping the lid off and exposing a bank of key holes.

"There are about twenty holes . . . and only four keys. How do I know which slots to put them in?" Isabella said, her voice rising with panic.

Jones ran back to the man who was making a weird motion with his eyes. He spun them around and then looked up, down, and then side-to-side.

55, 54, 53 . . .

Jones was totally baffled. "He's twirling his eyes then doing this up, down, side-to-side thing."

"Of course, the symbol," she said. She grabbed the keys, doing her best to steady her hands. Now that she stared at the bank she could see that they weren't laid there evenly, there was a circle pattern. She tried each key in the hole at the top of the circle. The final one fit and she pushed it in. She did the same at the bottom, then the two sides. Finally, she was able to make the keys fit.

23, 22, 21 . . .

"The keys are all in but they aren't working, they aren't doing anything!" She could hear the rising panic in her voice. She wanted to cry.

The man began jerking his head.

10, 9, 8 . . .

Jones looked from the man to Isabella. "TURN THEM! TURN THEM!"

Isabella prayed there was no special order. There was no time. Wait, the Crusaders were Catholics. Top, bottom, left, right . . . the sign of the cross. She started at the top.

As she turned the final key, the clock counted down to zero.

Chapter Twenty-Eight

Boom and Bust

Neil and Larry stared at each other and the chute that lay at their feet. Jeanne Valette stood on the edge of the railing and smiled. "The chute is a one-person model only. One person lives. Who will it be?"

Neil and Larry looked back to the stairwell. Plumes of smoke continued to rise from the hatch. "No going that way, partner," Larry said. "Unless you feel like getting grilled or poached."

"I think I'd taste better in a sauce," Neil said.

Larry smiled. "Now, that's way better banter. Too bad you left it so late."

"Stop chattering," Valette said. She looked at her watch. "You've got about three minutes before this building collapses in on itself. It takes about a minute to parachute down to safety."

Neil and Larry looked at each other. "We don't need any time to decide," they said together. Larry bent down and grabbed the chute.

Valette smiled. "So, the older cousin is the greedier cousin. Very good. If you ever need a job, and I know you will, look me up."

Larry looked at Neil. Neil nodded and together they walked back to the oscillating satellite dish and strapped the remaining parachute onto Jean-Claude Chili.

Valette grabbed her rip cord. "Seriously? Chili? That old coot has lived his life. He's not worth anything. He doesn't even have a family anymore."

Neil stood up angrily. "WHAT ARE YOU TALKING ABOUT?"

"His stupid sister in the bibliotecque? I'm afraid I had no choice but to kill her. She and her brother had set up websites to help you, phone numbers—and then showing you that book? They aligned themselves with the enemy, so they were my enemies."

Neil had had enough. He bent down and grabbed some stones and turned and ran straight toward Valette. "Let's see how well your parachute works with holes in it!" he yelled, loading up his gas mask.

Valette smiled. "See how strong you can be? I think you'll change your mind about that chute," she said, and she stepped backward and fell.

Neil reached the edge and watched as she flew down the side of the building, opening her chute and drifting down slowly, using her legs to push herself away from the glass. He threw the stones and mask after her.

He turned around. Larry was dragging Chili over to the edge. "Larry, we've got to wake Chili. He can't just drift down there unconscious; he'll crash."

"And if I know anything about the guy after spending the day with him, it's that he won't go unless we push him. He won't let us push him if he's awake. That's what's known as a conundrum, but I've got a plan."

They leaned Chili up against the railing. Larry tight-ened the straps, and then took off his belt and tied it to the release key for the chute. "Hold on to the belt until I say goose," Larry said. Then together they leaned him over the edge, holding him tight by the shoulder straps of the chute to make sure he didn't fall.

"I'm sorry about this," Larry said. He slapped Chili across the face. Chili woke up as if he'd been dunked into a tub of cold water. He looked around, confused.

"What eez zees, what eez happening?"

"Thank you for everything," Neil said.

"Remember to push yourself away from the side of the building," Larry said.

Chili looked down and saw the parachute. He also saw the Flambés weren't wearing any. An ominous rumble shook the building. "No, you cannot do zees! You must save yourself!" Chili wrestled to pull himself back up to the roof.

Neil and Larry let go of the shoulder straps and Chili began to fall. Neil held on to the belt and the chute engaged.

"Goose!" Larry yelled. Neil let go of the belt and Chili fell away from them toward the street. They watched as he pushed himself away from the windows. He was headed right toward the spot where Jeanne Valette's chute now lay abandoned.

Neil checked his watch. "He should just make it," he said. "Why did you want to yell goose?"

"I was sick of duck," Larry said.

They stared at each other for what seemed like an eternity.

"So . . . that wasn't a bad life, was it?" Larry smiled, slapping Neil across the back.

"No. It wasn't," Neil said. "Though I wish it had been longer." He'd faced life-and-death situations a number of times, but now that death was imminent, he felt an odd calm. He thought of his parents, Angel, Nakamura . . . Isabella. Isabella?

"Wait, didn't you say Isabella was here too?"

"Downstairs watching the guards. I hope she and Jones got out okay."

"I'm sure Jones did everything he could." Neil smiled.

Neil could see that police cars and fire engines were now gathering around the base of the building. "If Valette really did booby-trap this place, then those guys are in danger too."

Larry pulled out his phone and dialed Isabella. "You know, this phone is how I found you. The neat thing about this phone and yours is that they're linked."

"Linked?"

"Yeah, it's a special app I downloaded when we got them. I can always find your phone, no matter where it is."

"And I can find yours?"

"Uh, don't get crazy. Hmm, she's not answering."

"Dial 911."

Larry looked at Neil with a smile. "Um, it's 112 here, already dialed it."

Larry explained the situation to the police as they gazed over the edge. They watched as the police and firefighters quickly backed away from the building.

Neil turned to Larry. "No chance they could send a copter to get us?"

"Not enough time. I asked."

Neil watched as his watch ticked closer to what he presumed was zero on Valette's countdown.

"I bet there's a lot of crime evidence that's about to collapse with this building. It's too bad we won't be able to rat Valette out to the cops."

Larry grinned. "Funny story. I also downloaded an app that records everything on your phone. Voice-activated. I already downloaded the file and sent it to Nakamura. He'll get it to the proper international authorities."

"When did you do this, exactly?"

"While you were wasting your time chasing her over by the railing. You've got to let your anger go there, buddy."

"Too bad I'll never get a chance to use these incredible life lessons."

Larry grinned again and winked. "Really? 'Cause by my internal clock this building should have been reduced to rubble about ten seconds ago." He stood up. "I think it'll be better to end the curse the way it started, with the Flambés sending a crazy Valette to jail."

Larry's phone rang. "Looks like Isabella. You answer it." He handed the phone to Neil.

"Hey," Neil said. "Where are you? Are all right?"

"Neil!" Isabella said with a thrill, loud enough that even Larry could hear her. "You're safe!?"

"Yes, sort of. Better than expected, actually."

"We're okay too, Neil. We're okay. We shut off the bomb, Neil. Jones is going to get the police to send a helicopter up to get you. Sit tight, they'll be there soon. I can see Chili and the police on the other side of the glass. They're going to break down the door. I'll call you back."

Neil paused. Words were never his strength—he was better with food. "I can't wait," he said with a smile.

Chapter Twenty-Nine

Chili Weather

Jean-Claude Chili sat in his wheelchair next to Hugo Victoire's hospital bed, the remains of their shared croissant sitting on a dish. Hugo was sleeping. Chili was watching him with a wistful smile.

There was a light knock at the door. Chili looked over.

"Ah, Neil Flambé. *Venez*, come een." Chili wheeled his chair to his side of the room. "Don't worry. Hugo eez used to loud noises. I snore like a greezly bear, apparently."

"You've been together for a long time?"

"*Oui*. Many years." Chili gently smiled. "My sister, she eentroduced us when they were at culinary school togezer. We have been through many things. Of course, I deed not want him mixed up in zees. Or my sister. But they were both, how do you say, inseestant."

"I'm very sorry that I came here. You warned me, and I'm sorry I screwed things up so badly."

"I am also to blame. I knew zat zee 'orrible Valette was targeting you as soon as I visited your Chez Flambé zat day. Your food smelled and looked fabulous, but as soon as I tasted eet, zee food . . . eet turned to ashes. Zees was not . . . natural. I should have warned you, told you my suspicions. But I believed zat that I could fight her in Paris, and keep you safe. I apologize for zat as well."

"I don't understand how you even knew about the curse."

"Your great-grandfazzer. 'Ee was a great chef. So many of zee Flambés were. And zee Chilis have always been critics, even before zee Michelin guide. My grandfazzer, 'ee went in search of the greatest meal in zee world. Imagine his surprise when ee was told zat zee greatest chef in zee world was working in zis Cheektowaga, or whatever eet eez called. In zee United States? Pshaw. Impossible. 'Ee could not believe 'eet, so 'ee traveled to zees place. He arrived on zee very night that zee restaurant was destroyed by a great fire. Zee next day zee chef, he had vanished. My grandfazzer, 'ee searched zee ruins and 'ee discovered zees strange book. Inside were zees recipes for 'orrible foods—badger? Vulture? Chipmunk?"

"They are not as bad as you think," Neil said. "And they helped me beat the stupid computer."

"I weel take your word for eet. 'Ee brought zee book back home and one day 'ee give it to me, on a rainy day. I see zees strange messages appear on zee pages and I begin to ask zee questions. My sister, she is an expert on zees things and togezzer we put zee pieces into a puzzle. Then, when I met you zat day zat zee 'orrible Calamari tries to keel you, well, I knew you would need zees book someday. When you turn feefteen, like zee great Flambé chefs before you."

"I'm going to add my recipe for my *pommes de terre* into the final page when we get home. Maybe, if I have a family someday, my daughter or son might discover it on a rainy day."

There was another knock at the door and it opened. Chili looked up and a huge smile spread across his face. "And anozzer theeng I can tell you. Never underesteemate a Chili!"

Hortense Chili sat in her wheelchair, with Isabella pushing from behind. Isabella smiled as they came in the room. "We had a wonderful tea down in the cafeteria. Your sister is bouncing back very well."

Hortense patted Isabella's hand. "A sweet girl. You are very lucky." She nodded at Neil.

Neil blushed. "And thank you for all your help. I was just telling your brother how sorry I was to put you all at such risk."

"Sometimes it helps to be an expert in medieval medicines. Jeanne Valette was hoping my death would look like a heart attack, so she gave me a lethal dose of wolfsbane. I'm no idiot—I saw that coming a mile away—so I waited until she left, then swallowed some atropine, the only known antidote. It still almost killed me, and it was extremely painful, but it worked. Now she is in jail, thanks to my brother."

"Let us say zat I heet zee ground running, and zee wretched Valette deed not."

"A broken leg," Neil nodded. "When she landed on top of her pilot's body."

"I was able to track her down weetheen seconds. She deed not 'ave a gun zees time to even zee odds, and I was able to use a piece of zee 'elicopter rotor as an epee. Voilà. Togezzer we win zee day in zee end."

"She'll have a nice long time in jail to practice her fencing, I suppose." Neil smiled. "It's funny how the Valettes made all that money selling restaurant equipment and prefab food, and it still wasn't ever enough for them."

"Yes, zat was 'ow zay had such control over zee Flambés for so long. Zey steal all zee top jobs, all zee supplies from all zee others."

"A monopoly," Hortense said. "They worked behind the scenes of many organizations, bankrolling criminals and shadow businesses. The front of the door says one name but behind the scenes was always a Valette. You ordered their silverware, their air conditioner, without even knowing it was from them. Even we could not be sure."

"All starting with money they stole during the Crusades."

She nodded. "After the Crusades, they tracked down

Pierre Flambé and robbed him. They turned that money into their first endeavor, selling stolen salt and pepper to the Royal Court in Spain. They steal, then sell."

"But steal from whom?" Isabella said.

"From whomever they saw as an enemy. They pillaged the Holy Land, and later used the Inquisition to rob the people of Andalusia. There was a Valette sailing with the conquistadors as they attacked the Aztecs—and with the English explorers, and the French, and with Soviet tanks. Today, they continue to do these things. If there is a war, you can bet a Valette is there grabbing the local specialties."

"And to top eet off, zay are zee world leader in zee sales of frozen croissants and zee microwaved fish dinners. Ack. To pretend zat zay are somehow zee moral *boussole*, zee moral compass, for zee free world . . . Eet eez *pitoyable*, pathetic."

"We should leave you all to rest," Isabella said, walking up to Neil and taking his hand in hers.

"Once Hugo and I are releazed, we would love to 'ave you join us at our place for a wonderful dinner. Hortense eez zee real chef in zee family, of course."

"And I promise, no wolfsbane in my *Veloute de Volaille*."

"It is extremely tempting," Neil said. "If only so that I can steal your secrets. But I have a restaurant to try to save."

Isabella nodded. "Our flight is in just a couple of hours, in fact."

Neil walked over and kissed the Chilis on both cheeks.

"I thank you and my family thanks you. I just wish I could do more to show our gratitude."

"Pleeze. Go home and make zee great food again. Zees would please me above all else. You are a great chef. I am sure of zees. Make zee world a better place weeth your geefts. Zees is zee thanks zat I would like."

"I promise. And tell Hugo that I will meet him anytime in a head-to-head croissant battle."

Isabella squeezed Neil's hand.

"I mean charity fundraiser. We'll just fight for bragging rights."

Chili smiled. *"Bonne chance."*

Neil turned at the door. "Monsieur Chili. I have one last question."

"Oui, mon garçon?"

"I don't smell you. Angel didn't smell you all those years ago. I mean . . . I can smell the grease on the chicken cacciatore they are about to try to serve you for dinner, coming down the hallway."

"I 'ave already asked my friend Andre to head zem off at zee pass and bring us some cassoulet."

"Good. But my question is . . . if I can smell that, why don't I smell you?"

Chili tapped his own nose. "I am afraid zat eez a trade secret. Perhaps anozzer day." He smiled. "Don't worry. As I said before, I am certain we weel meet again. Until zen, perhaps a little mystery eez not necessarily a bad zing."

Neil smiled. "I've had enough mysteries for my fifteenth year, I think." He waved good-bye and quickly caught up to Isabella.

"You I can smell," Neil said. "And you smell wonderful." He could feel a lump in his throat. "And I don't ever want to put you in danger again."

Isabella smiled. "I like you very much, Neil Flambé, but I am not some kind of orchid. Let's see where the adventure takes us, okay?"

"Right now, I just want it to take me home."

"Well, your donkey is waiting for you, laden with gold."

"Seriously?"

"Of course not, what do you think this is, the Middle

Ages? Larry and Jones are waiting in the lobby with a cab . . . and a box of your favorite cheeses."

Neil grinned. "You know what? That's actually perfect, just perfect." Neil smiled and took Isabella's hand in his. Together they walked out into the sunlight.

Epilogue

Grand Reopening

A giant shadow passed over Chez Flambé, darkening the window that looked out into the alleyway. Neil Flambé poked his head out of the window and watched as the crows repeated their nightly migration. He spied an especially large black crow at the lead of the flapping mass of birds.

"Hmmm," Neil said, "I wonder what a crow would taste like in a tortiere?"

Larry joined him at the window. "I think you need four and twenty of them, not just one big fat one."

Neil smiled. "You offering to do a little hunting?"

Larry shuddered. "I thought the dead goose thing was creepy enough, thank you."

"So maybe we modern Flambés should just leave that kind of cooking in the past?"

"Now, *that's* a recipe for success," Larry said.

"Okay, back to work." Neil smiled and turned his attention to the fresh pile of clams on his counter. The crows continued to pass overhead outside, but Neil didn't see bad omens anymore, just crows being crows and enjoying a flight in the cool evening air.

"So Nakamura was telling me those critics really did get food poisoning, sort of," Larry said, walking over and began washing a savoy cabbage in the sink. "Something leeched in from the silverware, apparently."

"Mercury."

"Yikes. Not our fault, exactly. But that's still going to be a tough rap to bounce back from, regain the trust of the customers—that sort of thing."

Neil shrugged. "My dad says there's no such thing as bad press."

"I'm not entirely convinced that's true when 'poison' and 'food' are used in the same sentence."

Neil smiled. "We'll just have to be better than ever. No problem for me. And I have a few new recipes, including one for fresh croissants that I think will knock a few socks off."

The new fridge purred in the background, bought and installed with a thorough background check by Nakamura and the police. The Valette company—and its subsidiary DBC—still owned most of the market, even with the CEO behind bars, but there was no way Neil was going back to them.

"It was a good thing Nakamura smelled the gas."

"I didn't smell anything," Nakamura said, walking in the back door. He handed Larry a large mug of fresh coffee. "But I know what gas looks like when it's passing in front of, say, a blue motion sensor light. And when I realized Carbo was a fake, I put two and two together. . . ."

"And got methane."

"Yup, tanks full of the stuff were buried in a tunnel right under your restaurant. Doesn't smell like natural gas, but blows up just the same."

"Unless a superintelligent cop finds out about it in time," Larry said.

"Well, thanks." Nakamura smiled.

"I was talking about Stromboli."

"Ha, ha. Just for that, no more free coffee. So, Nose—what's on the menu tonight?" Nakamura reached for a slice of pecorino cheese.

"That is for the paying guests to find out," Neil said, slapping his hand. "And that cheese is measured perfectly for my sweet pea risotto, so back off."

"Paying guests? Isabella told me this was a charity event tonight."

Larry nodded. "It is. All the money is going to help that food bank where Angel works."

"You're kidding me. Are you trying to tell me that Neil Flambé isn't just about glory and profits?!"

"Yeah, just call him Phil Anthropy," Larry said.

"I see the puns didn't get any better after your little trip."

"Ha, ha. Neil isn't being completely altruistic. He's also invited all the food critics in the city over . . . for free. We're gonna wow them."

Nakamura stood up. "Well, it's always refreshing to see that not too much has changed. I only stopped by to pass along some good news. Picón was picked up about an hour ago."

Neil's head snapped up. "What? Where?"

"Singh actually found him—completely by accident.

He spotted Picón at a convenience store, trying to buy some lubricant for that weird suit he's wearing. I guess it got rusty in the water."

"He's still in that?"

"The guys at the station say it's hard to tell where the suit starts and Picón ends. I guess he had just enough time after DBC finally self-destructed to jump out. He still ended up in the water, but didn't sink with the van. He admits to getting your ID from the safe, by the way, so that closes the book on that."

"Thanks ever so much for your trust," Larry said.

Nakamura got up and walked toward the back door. "No problem. I'm sure I'll get another chance to charge you with something. Which reminds me, the coffee was five bucks." He smiled and walked out.

Larry threw a dime after him and then closed the door.

Neil watched Nakamura pick up the dime and wave good-bye as he walked away, shaking his head. Neil noticed something else, behind the garbage bin. "Larry, is that your motorcycle parked out there?"

"Yeah! Now that we're back in business I figured I could buy it back."

"What about the me-shirts?"

"I made a killing on those."

"Please don't say 'killing.'"

"Sorry, I made a bundle on them at City Hall last Friday—casual Friday, they call it."

"I don't follow."

"I printed up a hundred 'You're looking at the next mayor' shirts—went to the cafeteria and sold every last one. As long as no one reads anyone else's me-shirt, I should be fine."

There was a knock at the back door. It was a shaggy-looking bike courier. "I'll get that," Larry said.

"All right. Well, dinner service starts in about thirty minutes. I'm just going to say hi to the guests."

Neil took a quick tour of the dining room. He apologized to the food critics and thanked the many VIPs who'd shelled out a thousand bucks for the privilege of a real medieval feast. His parents had bought tickets, but called to say they couldn't make it until later.

Neil stood on one of the new chairs he'd been forced to buy. "Remember, tonight we eat with our hands. Huge joints of meat, suckling pigs, flagons of real handmade mead and ale—and those will be served by the much-older-than-me Angel Jícama."

"Just don't tell anyone about the barrels in my basement." Angel chuckled.

"And at the end of the evening, each of you will enjoy a special souvenir of the evening, an autographed copy of the menu, illuminated in gold by the wonderful Soba twins, Amber and Zoe."

"The gold is not edible," the twins said.

Neil saw the front door open. "And I see our special guests have arrived."

Isabella and Jones walked through the front door. Isabella was dressed in a flowing blue robe and golden crown. Jones walked in behind her, dressed as a gorilla-sized court jester.

"Oh, be more jovial," she said, spying the menacing scowl on his face. "Remember, it's for charity."

Jones lifted one side of his
mouth in a kind of smile, which
actually made him look more
frightening.

"If anyone laughs, I'll
crush them," he whis-
pered to Angel.

"I must get back to
the kitchen," Neil said.
"But let the feast begin!"

Isabella raised her
scepter and yelled.
"Yes, serving serf. We
do not wish to see you
again unless you are
bringing us food!"

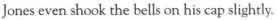

Jones even shook the bells on his cap slightly.

Neil and Isabella exchanged smiles and he walked
back through the kitchen doors.

He'd expected to see Larry plating the salads.
Instead, his cousin was sitting as still as a rock on one of
the stools, staring intently at a letter he held in his
hands. He looked shocked.

Neil ran up to him. "Larry, you okay?"

He turned to look at Neil. "Oh, hey, sorry, Neil, I
didn't hear you. Usually you yell."

"What the heck is going on? We've got dinner to
serve!" Neil yelled.

"Thanks. That's more like it. This is a letter from my
friend Hiro Takoyaki."

"Who?"

"Well, it's a bit of a long story. He and I write an online comic together. I write, he draws."

Neil had to shake his head to make sure he was hearing this right. "You write what? When? How?"

"Well, kind of all the time. I'm always jotting down ideas."

"In a kitchen?"

"Actually it's a perfect place for that. You see, the comic is about a superhero called . . . THE CHEF."

Neil blinked. Just this morning he'd caught Larry typing a long letter on his phone when he was supposed to be shucking peas. "This chef doesn't have red hair, does he?"

"No, I changed it to blond this morning." Larry quickly continued. "But here's the cool thing. The online comic biz doesn't really pay . . . unless you can get a book deal. Guess what?" He held the letter up with a huge smile. "WE GOT A BOOK DEAL."

Neil cocked his head. "Um, that's great. I think."

"And guess what else!" Larry held up a first-class plane ticket. "I'm going to Japan!"

"What? When? Tonight?"

Larry looked at the date on the ticket. "Next week!"

Neil found himself fighting an odd mix of emotions. Larry looked so incredibly happy, but he was also wondering if Larry had thought everything through.

"We do have a restaurant to run, you know," he said softly.

Larry walked over and slapped him on the shoulder. "I've already handled that. Look . . ."

He pointed to Neil's office door. The smiling bike courier walked out, buttoning up a white cotton chef's jacket. "Hey, you must be the boss. My name's Gary. How do I look?" he said.

Neil Flambé didn't say a word. Instead he turned to his cousin.

"Larry," he said.

"Yeah?"

"Before you leave, are you still taking orders for me-shirts?"

"I guess so."

"Good. I'll take one 'shoot me now' and one 'I'm with useless.'" Neil looked from Larry to Gary, who grinned at him. "On second thought . . . make it two."

Acknowledgments

Wow, whom to start with. I have to give the largest Neil Flambé hug to Michael Levine, my super-agent, who helped save our favorite teen chef from the shipwreck of the past year. To quote the great Stan Lee "'nuff said" about that. And a special thanks to Carolyn Forde at Westwood Creative for guiding me through the fine print.

Jon Anderson (a true champion of all things Neil!), Kevin Hanson, Alison Clarke, Felicia Quon, Rita Silva, Michelle Blackwell, and so so so many others welcomed Neil with open arms at Simon & Schuster. I bow down in thanks.

Ariel Colletti, editor extraordinaire, helped Neil get even better in the kitchen and on paper.

Laurent Linn made him look better . . . and Neil says he feels better too.

Katrina Groover and Michelle Kratz, the dynamic duo who rolled up their sleeves and helped get these books ready on time! Wow.

If I miss anybody, please know that it's just my exhausted brain hiccupping. . . .

I also want to thank all the musicians who keep me company while I write and draw. I sneak some of them into the books, of course. See if you can find them. This book was shaped by Arcade Fire and Great Lake Swimmers from start to finish, with healthy doses of Coeur de Pirate and Regina Spektor mixed in for good measure.

Thanks to all the artists who, like Neil and Isabella, strive to make the world a batter, I mean better and more beautiful place . . . and who all constantly seem to find themselves under attack. When the world is run by artists there's always a place for bean counters, but when the world is run by bean counters, they find no room for artists. Hmmmm.

Kevin Sylvester

is an award-winning writer, illustrator, and broadcaster. *Neil Flambé and the Marco Polo Murders* won the 2011 Silver Birch Award for Fiction. Kevin was particularly pleased by this because the kids vote! His other books include *Gold Medal for Weird* (Silver Birch winner in 2009!), *Sports Hall of Weird*, *Splinters*, and *Game Day*. He spends most of his time sitting in his attic studio, drawing and writing and listening to Neil and Larry arguing over, well, everything. He also loves to cook.